THRONE OF A PHARAOH

CROWNE LEGACY

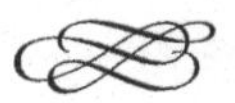

SHERELLE GREEN

Editor: There For You Editing

This one took a village, lol.

Thank you to sis for everything. Hubs for the brainstorming. Matysha for saving the day. Midnight for all your support. To my author crew for having my back always. And a special thanks to J & T for all the laughs & inspiration.

RECOMMENDED READING

To avoid any spoilers from previous titles, check out the following books:

Carter's #Undoing (To Marry a Madden)

Face Down Fridays (Crowne Legacy)

Sins of a Saint (Crowne Legacy)

To Marry a Madden (To Marry a Madden)

Jedidiah's Crowning Glory (Crowne Legacy)

Love Always, Tristan (Crowne Legacy)

Cheatsheet of the nicknames for the Crowne siblings that appear or are mentioned:

Saint (Scotch)

Hollis (Hennessy)

Creed (Cap)

Jedidiah (Jackie D)

Nash (Napoleon)

Pharaoh (Patron)

Keaton (Kentucky)

THRONE OF A PHARAOH

Ever get reacquainted with someone who made you become the hardened person you are?

HIM

She walked into the room like she owned it, demanding that I pay attention before she even voiced a word. When faced with the brown beauty, I almost forgot my number one rule:Trust No One. It's something I remind myself daily. We all have an addiction and if I'm not careful, she'll become mine. I can't afford any distractions right now, especially when my latest obsession has secrets that can do more harm than good.

HER

He has every reason not to trust me and yet, I can't help but be drawn to him in every way. How he speaks. The way he walks. The fact that all eyes are on him when he's in their presence. I can't recall a time in my life when I wasn't running from something, and not always by choice. I don't want to crave him like plenty of women already do. He's a Crowne. We'd never work. So why can't I seem to remember that fact whenever I'm near him?

DEAR READER

Wow, I can't believe this is my 40th story! From the first time Pharaoh was introduced, he stole my heart. Not just because he was a sexy ass Crowne, but because he loved his kids and I'm a sucka for a man who is good with kids.

Pharaoh is a boss and he needed a strong heroine who would keep him in check. As always, there are some surprise elements in this story and some new characters who had me smiling hard.

Buckle up as Crowne Legacy continues…

Much Love!

Sherelle

CHAPTER 1

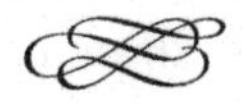

Fuck Weddings, Save Money

PHAROAH

I've been married three times.

Divorced twice.

Annulled once.

Engaged once more.

Had strong feelings for all my ex-wives.

Hated one of them.

Had several others propose to me.

Fell into a pussy or two.

Maybe more.

Fuck it. I fell into too many pussies to count.

Was the last dick for one before she decided men weren't for her.

Had the dice roll on deuce for how many times I'd been in love ... and not the surface stuff, but that deep, soulful shit. Would never admit how many didn't love me for the right reasons, nor would I confess how much that mess affected my outlook on relationships.

Yet, through all the court dates, restraining orders, DNA tests, baby momma drama, birthday gifts, crazy ex-husbands, child support checks I sent out every month, and other bullshit, I couldn't believe at damn near forty-five muthafuckin' years old, I still had kids poppin' up claiming I was their daddy.

"You walk around Chicago like you're entitled and I don't like you," the kid said, sitting across from me at the decorated wedding reception table that was as classy as Nash and Jade's wedding had been.

Fuck you, too, lil nigga. "You think I'm your dad, huh?" I asked, ignoring his comment.

"I don't think. I know." He crossed his arms over his chest, trying to show little emotion and failing to hide his nerves.

Damn. The little shit really did look like me. He still had to grow into his body, but he was gonna be tall. At least six-five like me. And he had my facial structure. Eyes. Jaw. My broad shoulders. Hell, he was even growing dreads like me.

Briefly glancing over at his mom, who was watching us from the dessert table, I went through my list of names. *Is it Gina or is it Gianna? No, it was Gia. Wait, I think Gia was her friend I wanted to sleep with. Ginger? Nah. Maybe Giselle? Um, nope. Matter fact, I think it was—*

"Genesis," the kid said, annoyingly clenching his jaw. "The least you can do is remember her damn name."

"Watch your tone," I warned, impressed that he was intuitive and analyzed my facial features enough to recognize I was trying to guess her name. "I remembered her name, but it's been a minute since I saw your mom." *And how did she even get invited to the wedding?* My brother, Nash, did have a lot of friends, but his wife, Jade, knew twice as many people and had been making friends with half of Chicagoland even though they lived in New York and frequented LA where Nash used to live.

"Last time you were with her was fifteen years ago," he said. "You requested a private dance from her, then you asked her out after. She was a stripper back then."

"You know a lot about me and your mom's relationship." *Especially since you're a kid talkin' 'bout grown folk's business.*

He laughed. "If you can call it that. You had sex with her, she got pregnant. By the time she got the nerve to tell you, you were with someone else. I'm fourteen by the way."

Not exactly how that happened. "I figured."

He shrugged. "Wasn't sure if you could do the math. Worst thing you can do is assume people know more than they do. You only get disappointed that way."

I squinted my eyes, observing him a little more. When Genesis cornered me before the wedding, she told me he was smart for his age. I could tell he was intelligent in our brief interaction today.

"What's your name?"

"Noble," he answered. "It was my grandfather's name. He was in my life since you weren't."

I didn't need to tell him that had I known about him, I would have been in his life. He didn't need to hear that, especially from a muthafucka who he didn't know yet.

"I assume you want a DNA test," he said.

"We don't have to talk about that now. I'm thinking we should meet for dinner sometime this week or next and get to know each other better."

"Yeah, right," he huffed, looking around the reception and fidgeting with an engraved napkin. "You expect me to believe that you wanna get to know me before knowing if I'm your kid? I heard you already got hella kids."

"How about Tuesday?" I asked, ignoring him once again. "I can pick you up or you can meet me at this joint in Hyde Park. Heard of Mesler restaurant at the Sophy Hotel?"

"I heard of it," he said. "It's where old folks meet up to shoot the shit, but they are tryin' to get some younger folks in there."

"It ain't that kind of place." I leaned slightly forward. "And I'm sure you've heard enough about me to know that I only do business in vetted places. You'll enjoy it."

He kept his expression neutral, sizing me up. "I guess it's cool if we meet up," he finally said, standing up from the table. He glanced out at the dance floor, the same direction he had before. I slightly turned to see what had his attention.

"Ah, I see why you keep looking around," I teased. "I guess she's prettier to look at than me, huh?"

He shrugged, with a slight smirk. "She's aight. Her name's Kennedy. We know each other from around the neighborhood, but I didn't know she would be here."

"My brother who just got married worked with her father in the past."

Nodding, he shuffled from one foot to the other, gripping the back of the bronze chair, looking just as nervous as he did when we first started talking.

"Why don't you ask her to dance?"

"She's already dancing with that funny lookin' dude."

I laughed, pretty sure that was one of my cousin's kids. Duchess had three siblings still living that we knew of, but we rarely saw her oldest brother, Charles, and his kids and grandkids. However, with the passing of my sister-in-law, Tristan, and now, Nash and Jade's wedding, we'd seen more family than we had in a while.

"She would rather be dancing with you," I pointed out, standing beside him, noting again how tall he was for his age. "You keep looking her way, but she's staring at you just as hard. You can stand here the rest of the night lyin' to me about how much you're feelin' her. Or you can do something about it and ask her to dance."

"She may say no."

"She won't." I gave him a slight nudge. "Go."

"I don't like being bossed around."

"Then quit stalling and go out there so I won't have to tell yo' ass what to do."

He gritted his teeth and pretended to brush down the sleeves of his dress shirt, but I knew he was shaking off his nerves. He only took a couple steps before turning back to ask, "Out of curiosity, exactly how many other kids do you have?"

Too damn many. "Let's save that conversation for another time."

He laughed. "I get it. You want time to count and make sure you don't leave any out, right?"

"Go ask the girl to dance," I told him, still laughing as I watched him approach her and the smile that filled his face when she said yes. He placed his hand on the small of her back, but slowly, his hand inched lower. *Yep. Looks like he's mine.* Young love. I was a sucka for romantic shit like that.

"For the record, I don't want you turning my son into a hoe," Genesis said, as she approached. She stood beside me, both of us watching Noble dance.

I glanced her way, noting how good she looked in her royal blue, tight-fitted dress with her burgundy and honey blonde highlighted hair pulled to the side, showing off the nice curve of her neck. She'd stand out anywhere. It was impossible not to when you looked as gorgeous as she did.

I'd been around the block a few times, but I was a sucka for a juicy ass and smooth melanin skin. Her caramel-brown tone taunted me to run a finger down the arm closest to me to see how she'd react.

She had dimples, but they weren't too defined, and her eyes were that sultry kind of almond-shape. The kind that hinted at a good time if you played your cards right.

"Why you gotta call me out when the shit ain't true?"

She lifted an eyebrow. "Once a playa, always a playa."

"I just got a way with kids, and he needed a push."

"Well, push less," she warned. "In this case, my son has your DNA, so you gotta be careful not to give him any more of your ways than he already has."

"I ain't do shit." I reached out my hands. "So it ain't even gotta be like that."

"But it is." She crossed her arms over her chest, but I ain't even take a peek at what she was working with. I knew women loved that shit, daring you to look and cursing your ass out if you did. Plus, I'd already been checking her out from afar after she approached me earlier, that dress fucking with my mind more than it should.

"You judgmental as hell considering you don't really know shit about me."

"I asked around."

I shook my head. "Uh huh. I'm sure you did. What I don't get is why you sprung him on me during my brother's wedding?"

"What does it matter?" she asked. "Is it because all your other kids are here, and you don't like your other baby mommas knowing you got another one? I'm sorry introducing your son to you today was such an inconvenience."

"Don't do that," I said. "Meeting Noble is not an inconvenience, but you and I both know approaching me before the wedding was only because you are into it with my ex-wife, Sheneeka, who also happens to be at this wedding."

"How do you figure that?" she asked, lifting a curious eyebrow.

"I've been watching you all day," I told her, leaving out the fact that I had to shake off my intense reaction to laying eyes on her again. "Sheneeka is usually up to some sneaky shit, but today, she's been on another level with it." I glanced over my shoulder and spotted Sheneeka fuming in a corner. "I heard her ex-boyfriend left her because he was in love with another woman, and I assume you're the woman I heard about that Sheneeka felt like wasn't on her level."

"It wasn't even like that between him and I," she defended. "Yeah, I used to date him, but that was a while ago and we're friends. Not that it's any of your business, but he had a problem and I helped him out. She jumped to conclusions, and now, she's been running her mouth about me all around Chicago. Ain't nobody got time for her BS, and she's messin' with the wrong one."

"So let me guess," I stated, leaning closer to her, briefly breathing in the spicy scent of her perfume, "you figured you'd come today, not just to tell me about Noble, but to get back at her by showing up today wearing a dress you knew would get my attention." I leaned closer to her ear, refraining from kissing the tattoo she had slightly behind her earlobe. "Which just so happens to be royal blue, one of my favorite colors."

"I haven't seen you in forever, and wouldn't even know your favorite color," she huffed, rolling her eyes and planting one hand on her hip.

"Women talk. I'm sure you knew." I let my eyes briefly roam over her again. "And it did. Get my attention that is. If Sheneeka happened to see my interest, all the better, right?"

She opened her mouth to call me out, but shut it quickly. "Whateva. I don't play games when it comes to my son, and it's my fault for waiting so long for you to meet each other. But your ex-wife is a real bitch, and yes, I noticed you checking me out, so yeah, it felt good to stick it to her."

"Hmm." Her eyes bugged a little when she got heated. I liked that shit. And I wanted to fuck her … bad. In my experience, going back to pussy you already had came with a busload of problems and maybe a kid or two. However, if I crossed paths with a woman who gave me that extra good feeling, one that seemed different than the others in ways I couldn't quite place off the jump, it was best for me to lay low.

"Anyway," Genesis stated, waving off our flirtation, "we can schedule a DNA test soon, but I don't want anything from you. Noble and I are good."

"If he's mine, I'll take care of him. I'm sure you already suspected that."

"I did," she said sincerely. "I also know you're a busy man with a lot of shit going on. Noble is in high school now and he needs his father-figure, but don't mistake me wanting my son to know his dad with me wanting your money. Trust, we good over here. This is just about Noble."

"I hear you, but I take care of what's mine."

I didn't miss the way her eyes briefly dropped to my lips when she announced, "I betta get back to my seat."

I couldn't help but watch her ass jiggle as she walked away. *Shit.* She spelled trouble, but if Genesis wasn't careful, she'd get it again. Not sure how long I was staring her way before I felt someone pop me across the back of my dreads.

"Damn, Keaton, why'd you do that shit?"

"Because we've been texting in the group message for the past five minutes for you to join us for a quick meeting in the bridal suite, but yo' ass out here picking up baby mommas like they stray dogs."

"It ain't my fault I didn't know about this one until today."

She rolled her eyes. "That's something a nigga like you would say. Can you just come on so we can get back to enjoying the reception? Nash will get curious if the rest of us are gone too long, but Duchess told us to hold the meeting without her and Stan."

I ignored all the curious eyes looking my way as we dipped out of the main ballroom. Partly because there was too much eye candy to distract me and I had too many baby mommas in the room to move the way I wanted to.

It wasn't lost on me that Nash and I were always arguing about something, and he probably invited all my exes as some kind of sick, twisted joke.

"If it isn't Mr. Super Sperm himself," Hollis announced when I entered the room after Keaton.

"Fuck you," I spat, walking past Jedidiah who had his girlfriend, Korie, in his lap.

"What the fuck are y'all doin?" I asked, wondering why they were all nodding their heads when there wasn't any music playing, especially Hollis who was dancing, too.

"I gotta say, this the funniest shit y'all have come up with in a while," Saint said, pulling his fiancée, Taraj, to him, gently wrapping his arm around her pregnant belly.

I stood by Creed who hadn't cracked a smile all night. "Bruh, what the hell are they up to?"

"Some shit I refused to participate in."

"Participate?"

I hadn't even noticed they each had in one earbud until they began removing them, and the instrumental to a song started playing on the Bluetooth speaker Hollis had in his hands.

Taking out my phone, I sent out a quick text message for some business I needed to handle ASAP, preferably right after my siblings finished pissing me off, which I knew they would as soon as I recognized the song.

"Is this 'What These Bitches Want' by DMX?"

"Hell yeah," Hollis confirmed.

"Y'all doin' that DMX challenge or sumthin?" I asked. "That shit was poppin' years ago."

Keaton shook her head. "Nah, bruh. Not the challenge. We made up something of our own to the beat."

What the fuck does that mean? "Whateva the fuck y'all tryin' to do, do it fast. I got a business meeting soon."

"You always workin'," Hollis stated. "Do you really have to be all up and through the streets of Chicago when you ain't even got a drug shipment coming in?"

I shook my head. "Spoken like a muthafucka who don't appreciate what the fuck I do."

He raised his hands. "I'm just thinking about your health, bruh. Too much work can kill you."

Letting off the gas may kill me first.

"Did you start yet?" Jade asked, bursting through the room with the train of her wedding dress in one hand and the sleeve of Nash's shirt in the other.

"You're just in time," Korie told her, taking out her phone.

"What are you recording for?" I asked, already thinking about calming sounds in my head, a tactic a meditation specialist I used to fuck told me about years ago.

"Imagine my surprise when I got wind that you had another woman out there we ain't know about," Nash stated, standing on top of a chair. "It seemed cosmic in a way."

This dude. "Get to the point."

"P, do you remember when you poured that laxative in my drink during my engagement party?" Nash asked. "Had Jade thinkin' I shit my pants when I'm nervous."

Aw, shit. "You had it comin'. Is that why you invited most of my exes to your damn wedding?"

"It was," he confirmed, wearing a smile so obnoxious I wanted to punch the shit out of his preppy ass. "And to top off this glorious day of watching you dodge baby mommas left and right, we created a song for the occasion."

"We figure after having so many in the same room, you don't need a reminder of how many women you'd been with," Hollis added. "But you're gonna get one anyway."

Jade started beat boxing, and had it not been at my expense, I would have been impressed.

"What they really want from a Pharoah," Saint rapped.

"Somebody let him know," Jedidiah yelled.

"Jackie D, not you, too," I groaned, to which he just shrugged.

"Korie wanted to play along and I can't tell her no."

"Man, yo' big soft—" I was cut off by them turning up the beat and Hollis blurting out some shit that had me looking to Creed in disbelief.

"Tell me they didn't."

He frowned. "They did."

(Hollis) There was Francine, Kesha, Laura, Lesha. Michelle. Lorell. Ciera and Misha.

(Nash) Paula, Donna, Suzanne, Leah.

(Hollis) Sharon, Dottie, Zoey, Mia.

(Nash) Sheneeka. Yo, H, ain't that the crazy one he married before we met her?

(Hollis) Nah, she was the golddigger. Crazy one was named Poinsetta.

(Keaton) Never trust those women named after flowers, I'm telling you.

(Nash) Then there was Gabby, Abby, Sheena, Katreena.

(Hollis) About three Ashleys.

(Keaton) And Lashay, or was it Lena?

Nash shook his head. "Don't matter. He fucked both those twins."

"Not at the same time!" I interjected, sounding dumb as hell, but still wanting to defend myself.

"Bruh, we don't believe your claims," Keaton word-sang. "You be lyin'."

(Hollis) Like he tried to lie about being with Roxanne, Cheyanne, Trina, and Serena.

(Nash) Vaughn, not Dawn. Rita, not Denna.

(Keaton) Yo, didn't both of them claim he was they baby daddy?

(Hollis) Yep! The boy was named Blake and the daughter was Maddie.

"But I wasn't," I clarified. "I didn't mind being their father, but they have great men raising them now."

"That's good," Nash said with a smirk. "Because then you fucked with Jada. Deja. Stacy and Terri."

(Hollis) Shawnice, Latrice, and sweet southern Sherry.

(Keaton) Two of them got knocked up, but we love our nieces.

(Nash) Oh, let's not forget Porsha.

(Keaton) And grandma Queenie loved Peaches.

(Nash) Candy and Jasmine, with an *I* and a *y*.

(Hollis) Kayla. Navaeh.

(Keaton) That's the one that always cried.

(Nash) Lastly, Shawna and Mickey. Treya, then Vickie.

(Keaton) Oh shit, y'all! We almost forgot Ricki!"

"Damn, I did forget about her," Saint said.

"Ricki wit her clingy ass!" Hollis walked around the room, pretending to have dead weight on his leg. "I swear I saw her pop up months after the marriage was annulled." Hollis looked from Korie to Jade. "She like women now, though, and she's married to a little fine sumthin. Bruh forced her to go to the other side." Hollis hit Nash on the shoulder. "But she had a fat ass though, right? P should have called her Judy."

Nash shook his head. "I am a married man now, Hollis. I will not look at another fat ass. Talk about another ass. Think about another ass besides my wife's fine ass." He gripped Jade through her dress. "So I cannot confirm nor deny that P should have called her Judy with the big booty instead."

Jade laughed and playfully hit his shoulder. "You play too much!"

"Are y'all muthafuckas done messin' around?" I asked, my arms crossed over my chest.

Nash shrugged. "I guess. I think you got more exes, but I had to work on my wedding vows and the shit was taking too long to round them up."

"He looped me in," Hollis explained. "But I had to pass the rap to Keaton since lookin' at yo' list of exes just reminds me how slim the pickings are in Chicago if I'm tryin' not to fuck with the same women my brother messed with."

"Well, I didn't finish because working on this list just reminded me that I need to start knocking out some Christmas gifts for my nieces and nephews early," Keaton chimed in. "I swear, I have no fuckin' idea how you keep all those child support payments straight."

Usually, I was always down for a good laugh, even at my own expense, but a muthafucka was tired, and jokes or not, today had been exhausting juggling my exes in one place. I hated to admit it to myself, but I was grateful when Nash and Jade excused themselves to go back to the reception and the rest of my siblings started talking about the babymoon Saint and Taraj had took.

Shit. I needed me a damn vacation. All these kids and I ain't never heard of a babymoon before Taraj started telling us about that shit.

"You good?" Creed asked.

"Yeah, bruh, I'm good. Just got shit to do and these streets don't sleep." I dabbed fists with him. "Tell these assholes I slipped out to handle business."

Creed nodded. "I got you."

I left out of that room, dodged going through the reception all together, and walked out of the whole damn building with three things on my mind.

One, my family wasn't shit sometimes and payback was about to be a bitch. These mugs act like I ain't who the fuck I am, but that's how we all were with each other.

Two, son or not, Noble had been right. I really needed to keep better track of how many damn kids I had.

And three, no matter how great I was at masking my true feelings to conceal the truth from my friends, family, and especially my enemies, even a master could meet his match when he least expects it. Question was, had I already met mine?

CHAPTER 2

Fuck Exes, Stay Single

PHAROAH

Twenty minutes later, I was no longer able to maintain the façade as I pulled down an alley I knew like the back of my hand, parked my McLaren dark Sarthe Gray 720S Le Mans special edition sports car, and approached the green door already opening for my arrival.

"PDawg, do I need to tell you what a bad idea this is?" my security guard, Jock, asked, letting me pass. He was more than muscle though. He was my younger brother by a year. Different moms, same father.

"Nah, I knew I had fucked up hours ago."

Jock rarely called me out on shit, so when he did, I was in deeper than I realized.

"You need me to park the ride?"

I nodded, tossing him the keys. "Yeah, underground for me if you can. I just need to wrap this up." I had three main places I lived throughout Chicago, one spot being down the street with a secure underground parking garage. Jock wouldn't be gone long, but other men were in the facility if anybody who'd seen me pull up tried any funny shit.

My strides were long and purposeful as I walked down the narrow hallway, pulling up my dreads high on my head so they weren't in my face. Tugging off my tie, my adrenaline was pumping.

When I reached the back room, I shut and locked the door, before cracking my neck and taking a seat in my high ebony chair gilded in gold, a gift from an OG I used to look up to.

"I feel like I tolerate a lot of shit," I voiced, pulling out my Glock and placing it on the table, my hand close enough to the trigger in case shit popped off. "But I've killed a muthafucka for less before."

Genesis sighed, maintaining her stance in the corner of the room. "It's really not fair that Jock took my gun when I got here, so I'm vulnerable if you try something."

"When the fuck did you get back to Chicago, and why the hell didn't I know I had a kid?"

She looked at the gun, her apprehension obvious only to a muthafucka that knew her. Reluctantly, I placed the gun in the drawer.

"Explain yourself."

"Sending me a message demanding that I be waiting here when you arrived is hardly a smart idea," she huffed, crossing her arms over her chest.

"Ginx, stop stalling."

Her eyes softened for a second, no doubt because I

used my nickname for her. "I've been in and out of the city for the past eight months," she admitted. "Before that, just for quick trips."

I grinded my teeth together. "It's been years since we've seen each other, and you didn't think to tell me shit?"

"You wouldn't understand," she claimed, her voice slightly rising and the vein in her forehead popping, the first sign that she was uncomfortable.

"I wouldn't understand what exactly?" I repeated, standing from my desk, not stopping until I was in front of her. "Why you dropped off the face of the Earth years ago? Or why you popped up at my brother's wedding acting like our history wasn't as complicated as the fact that I have a goddamn son you never told me about it?"

"I'm not talkin' to you when you're like this."

"I earned a right to have answers, especially when you acted like we were practically strangers."

"We are now," she said.

"Do you know Jade?" I asked. "Is that how you got invited to the wedding?"

"No, a friend invited me last minute. If I'd had more time, I would have approached you before the wedding."

"A friend you fuckin' besides Sheneeka's man? Shiddd, I ain't know you still get down like that."

She reached up her hand to smack me, but I caught it and held on until she yanked it away. "You will not disrespect me and I'm not fucking your ex-wife's man. I don't have to explain myself to you!"

"The hell you don't," I spat. "Had a nigga needing to pretend like he wasn't surprised to see you when you know damn well I was shocked."

"You betta watch who the fuck you talkin' to like that." She poked my chest, her matte-polished acrylic nail sharp, but not sharp enough. "I am not the woman you used to know, and I damn sho' won't stand here and be scolded by you when I'm a grown ass woman."

"Ginx, you ain't on my level when it comes to being ruthless, so actin' hard will only piss me off."

That was a lie. I loved me a badass woman, and Ginx had always been a temptation of mine that I didn't understand.

"Piss you off, huh?"

Fuck. I must have shown a weakness because she adjusted her hair and flashed me that Ankh tattoo symbol right behind her ear, the one she knew I loved kissing. Her eyes sparkled with defiance, and I prayed she didn't look down at my slacks. Between the wedding and being here with her now, it was getting harder by the second to hide how much I was still attracted to her.

Genesis had always been a trigger for me. Jock knew it and so did my boys, Cash and Keon. We'd fooled around, but crazy enough, I only fucked her one night. *And that's all it took for her to get pregnant with my son.*

As badly as I knew I should stop whatever was about to happen before it did, I felt torn between wanting to take a step back or let shit play out.

"Did you miss me?" she asked, her fingers roaming along the outside zipper and button of my pants before she undid the bindings and her soft hand cupped my dick.

"Shit." I didn't answer because the truth may cause more damage than a lie, and she'd see right through my lie. That's how it had always been with us. Years or not, Genesis still had an MO when it came to me. It was a power struggle, me wanting to get her to concede and answer my questions, and her doing what she could to conceal her truth and distract me with my weakness … her.

I could spot a fucked-up situation a mile away, and as

wrong as it was to stand there and let her drop down into a squat position, I didn't stop her as the heels of her strappy royal blue stilettos slightly lifted off the floor as she got comfortable. Sucking my dick was a way of getting me to comply to her terms when she knew I was dead set on figuring out why shit wasn't sitting right.

My fucking sanity at this point? Questionable.

Her wearing my favorite color, squatted, with her lips on my dick? Stunning.

I'd missed her tongue. I'd lost count of how many times I imagined the way her filthy mouth suckled my balls before doing this suction thing that had me stumbling as she pushed me into the wall opposite of where she'd been standing.

When it came to sucking dick, women often fell into three categories: Hollywood Flop, Tasteless Tease Tanya, and Deep Throat Diva.

The Hollywood Flops pissed me off the most. They were the women that made it seem like they were dick-sucking champs. Yet, they were all show and no follow-through, often making a grand production of sucking it, but was clueless as hell. Not only did you not know what the fuck she was doing, but your dick was confused, too, chasing a release that may never happen due to lack of technique. Hollywoods needed a guidebook because the right side of her mouth never knew what the left side was doing.

Then there were the Tasteless Tease Tanyas. Every man liked a little playfulness. But when a Tanya takes too damn long teasing it with her tongue like she doesn't want to taste it, only to speed through the act when she finally puts you in her mouth, the shit kills me. How can you act like it's a muthafuckin' race and bite me in the process? Ain't you the same chick who was talking about "I don't like how it taste," but you want me to taste you? Nah, fam. Those were the ones that usually ended with you bandaging your shit up. Last one I encountered made me want to slap my dick across her face, zip my shit back up, and walk the fuck out.

And then there was my favorite kind. The down for whatever, whenever Deep Throat Divas. Those sexy sirens with limitless skills, hollow throats, warm and proficient tongues that left no nerve on your dick untouched. The kind of woman who was so skillful, you had to hold back busting a nut, her mouth game so damn good, you found yourself grabbing onto anything—her head, her hair, the wall—to brace yourself for the ride, anxious to see what unexpected thing her mouth would do next and how deep she could take you. A love-the-gag DTD never disappointed and would pop a cough drop to soothe her throat before letting you walk out the door unsatisfied. You would think this type was plentiful, but even though you could find a decent DTD, top-notch DTDs were rare.

Ginx was my first DTD.

She fucked me up for other women.

And any man who claimed to have the willpower to say no to a Deep Throat Diva was a goddamn liar.

* * *

GENESIS

I HAD him where I wanted him the minute he walked into the room. Throughout my entire childhood, I'd heard stories that you never forget your first love. The kind of love that even if the relationship wasn't the healthiest, it was innocent in ways future relationships never would be.

Falling in love with Pharaoh changed me forever. Yet, even now I wasn't sure if he knew he'd been my first love.

Pharaoh had always been the man that every woman in Chicago wanted, every man in the hood wanted to be, and every criminal feared, not because he was the most ruthless, but because an intelligent thug was the worst combination. He'd never been driven off emotion, only logic. If you earned his loyalty, you had an ally for life. If you broke his trust, your children's grandkids would remain an enemy.

What I was doing right now should feel so wrong, yet it felt so right. Pretending like we didn't remember each other at the wedding may have pissed him off, but I enjoyed the stolen glances he shot my way and the unforgiving look in his eyes that warned me he'd tired of whatever game I was playing before I'd even began playing it. It felt like the day I met him. A day I still cherished more than he realized.

"Ginx, this conversation ain't over," he groaned, his hands cupping the back of my head, no doubt fucking up my hair. I knew what he liked. Where he wanted my tongue. How much pressure he needed. When to suck and when to lick.

I anticipated the moment his body jerked, refusing to let up and swallowing as much as I could, careful to avoid letting any slip past my lips and onto my dress.

He didn't recover right away, his dark eyes part angry, part turned on, all sexy. I went to help him clean up and zip back his pants, but he turned, not giving me the opportunity.

I stood, smoothing out my dress and fluffing out my hair. He'd returned to his desk, not even looking at me as he took out an iPad and leaned back in his chair. I needed to make an exit, but not before I finally told him, "I'm sorry."

He looked up from his iPad. "For Noble or the other shit?"

"All of it."

He laid down the iPad and rubbed his beard, a stoic expression on his face. "Guess you should get back to the reception to get Noble?"

I felt dismissed even though I'd been planning to leave anyway. "My friend is staying with us while she's in town, so she'll take him back and I'll meet them there."

He nodded, but I didn't miss the slight peek of relief in his eyes before he masked it. *He looks better than I remember.* A younger Pharaoh had been gorgeous, but now, he was a grown ass fucking man with grey in his full dark brown beard, lips I wanted to ride into next Sunday, and long locs begging to be pulled.

He'd filled out, too. His body type changed to support broad shoulders, thick thighs, and muscular arms that were visible through his dress shirt. Gingerbread dipped in rich chocolate colored skin still smooth even with his scars. How he managed not to look like the struggles he'd faced in life were beyond me.

He was a whole royal vibe. An Egyptian god who already stood out by his name, yet, add his looks to that and he was downright lethal. It was easy to become mesmerized by his presence, but a knock at the door distracted me from admiring him more.

"Jock will escort you out," Pharaoh announced, extending an arm Jock's way. "Noble and I have plans to meet up this week. I trust that you're fine with him arriving on his own."

In other words, Genesis, I'll let you know when I'm ready to see you. "That's fine."

"Good."

Walking out of the building, I couldn't deny that his dismissal didn't sting a little, but I deserved it. I hadn't just hurt him by leaving, I hurt his pride, and if there was one thing I knew about men, it was that bruising their ego could cause irrevocable damage if the hurt was left unresolved.

Keeping Noble from him wasn't right, but I couldn't change the past. He hadn't seen me in years, and I didn't expect him to understand where I was coming from, but there was so much more of our story that he didn't know.

"Be easy, Genesis," Jock stated, holding open the door for me to leave.

"Thanks, Jock. You too."

The walk to my car that I'd parked around the corner felt nostalgic and suffocating at the same. Life had a funny way of keeping you humble, but my mother always said that the truth was more valuable when it took you a few years to find it.

Maybe if Pharaoh wasn't a Crowne, things would be different. Maybe if Duchess wouldn't have learned my secret and told me it was best I stay away from him, I would have told him about Noble.

Or did it all stem from the fact that all the maybes in the world couldn't hide the truth? That he'd been better off without me in his life, and now that I was back, he had no idea the hurricane that was coming his way.

CHAPTER 3

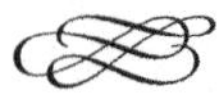

Fuck Snitches, Trust No One

PHAROAH

I believed in karma, but who the fuck had time to wait around for karma to show up and take action? Over the years, I'd learned to take shit into my own hands. Yeah, I had guys to do the dirty work, but I preferred to handle most business myself.

"How'd it go?" Jock asked, returning after escorting Genesis out.

"It is what it is," I answered nonchalantly. I wasn't fooling him though. If there was anyone who saw through my bullshit, it was Jock.

"Troy and Dex just arrived," he informed me. "Cash and Keon are watching them in the red room. Figured you ain't want them going too far until you got done with Genesis."

"Appreciate it. You can send them in."

They entered, both wearing the same arrogant, smug expression on their face as they usually did, except this time I peeped apprehension, too. *As they should be.*

"Take a seat, fellas." I pointed to the two seats across my desk, my eyes briefly looking to the wall as I thought about how Genesis had been squatting with my dick in her mouth ten minutes prior.

"I'm assuming you remember why I asked you here?"

Dex nodded. "Yeah, we do."

"Good." I opened my left drawer and pulled out a contract, taking a second to go over my goals once again in my mind. I didn't understand this younger generation of disloyal gangsters with an ego bigger than their valor. Therefore, ensuring I'd created the best plan of action was crucial.

"Everything we previously discussed is detailed in this agreement," I told them. "You'll be working with Cash and Keon just like you did on the UK shipment and the one before that."

Troy and Dex were cousins and DEA informants out of Detroit. They were the worst kind of traitors because the folks they ratted out had been their own fathers. The price on their head was steadily rising, so when they escaped to Chicago, my first instinct was to turn them over to Troy's younger brother, Titus, who had taken over the drug trade after his father and uncle got locked up.

Usually, I'd never do business with snakes, but with the DEA hot on my ass right now, Troy and Dex served a purpose I deemed more important than betrayal … security.

I offered them protection, and in exchange, they

continued to work as informants for the DEA. Only this time, they only disclosed information that I wanted law enforcement to know. Shit to keep them going in circles for that big fish to fry.

Regardless, anything I did was a temporary distraction. I would always be on the lookout, strategizing to distract the DEA, FBI, and CIA from pinning too much shit on me. In the streets, they called me Patrón. But unlike some of my Crowne siblings who were only known by their liquor nicknames, most knew me as Pharaoh Crowne. It was hard to keep shit discreet when you'd been in the game as long as I had with too many kids and exes to keep straight.

I slid the contract across my desk, giving them both a chance to review my terms. They knew the overall conditions were simple. Fuck me over and be killed. Succeed, and buy back your freedom. I fucking *hated* having anyone work for me who had proven to be untrustworthy. The shit never sat right, but I knew what I was doing.

I wouldn't have survived in this business this long if I hadn't kept my enemies close.

"We need time to discuss before we sign this shit," Dex stated.

"Nah." I linked my fingers in front of me. "You knew this was coming, and unlike y'all punk asses, I respect Titus. Only reason him and his crew ain't bombarded Chicago to drag y'all asses back to Detroit is because he doesn't want to make an enemy out of me. But make no mistake, you won't leave here without signing."

Troy was the first to glance over his shoulder and notice that Cash, Keon, and Jock were standing in the back of the room. I let out a forced laugh because we collected their guns at the door, so they were here without protection, but hadn't even peeped my men were in the back until now.

Another reason I couldn't stand these babyface wannabe thugs. When they snuck into Chicago, it had only taken five minutes of interrogating Troy and Dex to realize they were some coward ass muthafuckas who turned on their fathers because they wanted to be the top pit bull, when at their core, they had the grit of a Chihuahua.

Troy was the most annoying since he was built like a linebacker, but couldn't fight for shit. Not the way he needed to... with his brain, and not just his muscle. His older brother, Trent, was killed a few years back and his pops named his brother, Titus, as his successor. Dex wasn't any better, pissed at his dad for wifeing up the woman he'd loved since high school. It was fucked up, but clearly, daddy fucked her better than son.

Instead of supporting the chain of command, Troy and Dex accepted a deal from the DEA, too dumb to think of the consequences or the fact that Titus would make it his mission to have his brother and cousin pay.

"Is there a problem?" I asked, after Troy and Dex shared a look.

"No problem," Troy said, signing on the dotted line before handing the pen to Dex to sign.

"I'll be in touch soon," I informed them, motioning for Jock and Cash to escort them out.

"You good?" Keon asked me. "Heard Genesis is back."

"I'm good," I lied. "Don't know why the fuck she's back in town, but it turns out her son, Noble, may be mine."

He nodded. "I heard that, too. Can't believe she'd bring him to the wedding though."

"Me neither, but I know that kid does look like mine. Kinda reminds me of how Porter looked at his age."

Porter was my oldest son and Keon's godson, so Keon had a soft spot for him. When Keon didn't say shit else, I told him, "Might as well spit out whateva is on your mind."

"Just be careful," he warned. "Folks out there always lookin' for your weaknesses. That's why we keep your kids under as much surveillance as we can, and the ones we can't protect, we teach to hold their own." He cleared his throat. "But Genesis is different."

"She is," I agreed.

Keon left it at that, but he didn't need to say more. In my line of work, I'd watched drugs become a personal hell for many. What started out as a liberating release conformed into an entrapment of their stable mind when the drugs began making their crucial life decisions.

It was an addiction they didn't see coming as their need to escape reality became a necessity, not a leisure. It was the part of the job I hated to see, but everyone in the world was on drugs whether they realized it or not.

Their job was a drug.

Sex was a drug.

Their relationship was a drug.

We were all addicted to something that could be the cause of our demise. As fucked up as it sounded, Genesis was my heaven, until she became my personal hell. She was my drug of choice.

* * *

GENESIS

"Hey, Mom," Noble greeted me when I walked into the condo.

"Noble, I'm so glad you're up."

"I thought you may want to know how my talk went at

the wedding, so I stayed up."

I smiled, grateful that this kind, brilliant and handsome kid was mine. "I'm sure meeting Patrón today was unexpected, but he told me you're getting together with him this week to get to know each other."

"I know we need the DNA test," Noble stated, "but that piece of paper is only going to tell me what I already know. He's my dad."

I nodded, gently squeezing his arm. "He is, but this is a lot for you to take in."

"I can handle it, Mom," he confirmed, already standing several inches taller than me, but straightening his posture.

"Sweetie, you're the toughest kid I know, but it's okay if it's overwhelming. Just like it's fine if you would rather go back and live with Uncle Grey since I may have to leave Chicago again soon."

"I'll live here for as long as you're here," he said. "Uncle Grey could probably use the break anyway. He took the breakup with Cheyanne harder than he let on, but I think he's dating somebody new now."

I raised an eyebrow. "Oh really? How long has he been dating her?"

Last time I was in town for a few weeks, Grey had asked me to help out at his bakery, Brewed Awakening, and I met his girlfriend, Cheyanne. She was sweet, but I knew that Grey was feeling her much more than she was him.

While Noble gave me the 411 on Grey's love life, I couldn't help but feel a little guilty that Pharaoh was only just now meeting his amazing son, even if certain circumstances kept me away.

He'd be even more pissed if he found out his son was raised right here in Illinois. Grey was my cousin, but we were close, so

Noble lived with him and he grew up with calling Grey uncle.

He was just getting to the part where he'd caught the woman sneaking out of Grey's room when his phone rang.

His eyes lit up, but he tried to play it off. "Ma, it's Kennedy. Do you mind?"

I smiled, wondering when my adolescent, talkative son became a young man who was getting calls from girls. "Go ahead. I have to check on Destiny anyway."

I stifled a laugh when Noble answered with a nonchalant, "Whassup," as I walked down the hallway to the guestroom hoping Destiny was still awake.

"It's about damn time you got home," she squealed, opening the door before I even had a chance to knock and pulling me inside.

"Damn, Des. I wasn't even gone that long."

"You were gone long enough!" she exclaimed. "You see Noble's dad for the first time in years, and after role-playing like y'all ain't know each other, he demands you meet him during the middle of the damn wedding reception, and you wonder why I'm on the edge of my seat? I swear, sis, I was too glad Adrian couldn't attend Nash's wedding with me. Otherwise, I wouldn't have been able to witness what went down today."

From what Adrian, Destiny's husband, had told us, Nash used to live in LA—one of the places I called home—before he recently moved. Adrian had met Nash during his early street fighter days. Adrian still fought on occasion, but not as much.

"Girl, spill the tea already!" Destiny exclaimed when I was taking too long to respond. Since Des was an undercover reporter, she lived for juicy shit like this.

"My life is not one of your stories, Des."

"Say less." She waved me off. "I would never write about you and jeopardize your trust like that."

I smiled, grateful that I confided in Destiny all those years ago. Back when I didn't trust a soul and life seemed to be crumbling around me. In a way, being Noble's mom helped me center myself again.

"So?"

"So what?" I asked, taking a seat beside her on the bed.

"Girl, are you serious? What the fuck happened tonight?"

I sighed, untying my stilettos, then leaning back on the bed. "Well, I got there before he did. His emotions were high. My nerves were shot. He asked me a lot of questions that I wasn't ready to answer. And then …" I trailed off as I thought about how sexy he looked.

"Imma kill you!" Destiny yelped. "Enough with the dramatic pauses. And then what?"

"I wasn't pausing for dramatic effect," I disclosed. My eyes focused on the rotation of the ceiling fan as I realized, "Even with everything that has happened and what I know is yet to come, being with him today was the most alive I've felt in a while. It don't make no damn sense, since you and I both know I have no problem fulfilling my needs with whatever dude is appealing to me when that time hits. I can't afford to get into anything serious. I never could. Which is why I never should have sucked his dick today."

"Bitch, what?" she exclaimed before I motioned for her to calm down. The last thing I needed was Noble hearing this mess. "I'm sorry for getting loud, but I thought you were gonna tell me y'all kissed since you said he's the best kisser you've ever been with."

"He is."

"But you didn't kiss him?"

I shook my head. "Nope. I needed to gain some

ground after he was obviously and rightfully pissed at me, so I did what I had to do."

"What you wanted to do," she corrected.

I shrugged. "So maybe I've been thinking about sucking his dick ever since I started traveling back to Chicago. No biggie."

"Genesis, even though you have no problem being sexually liberated with a man, it's rare that you put yourself in a vulnerable position, and I can tell from your facial expressions that you're nervous about what having Pharaoh in Noble's life means for you."

I closed my eyes, pushing back thoughts that were too painful to even think. As much as I confided in Destiny, there was still so much she didn't know. Secrets I could never tell her for her own safety.

"I know there's more to your story," she said. "I guess I've realized since the day we met that there were layers to your past that I couldn't know."

"It's not because I don't trust you."

"I understand that," she said. "But whatever it is, if you don't want to entrust that information with me, then figure out if there is someone in this world you can trust. Maybe Grey ..." Her smile was filled with concern. "Maybe Pharaoh?"

"I didn't want to answer his questions today, but I do need to talk to him privately after he's had time to adjust to me being back," I admitted.

"Just don't give him too much time," she suggested.

I pinned her with my *really friend* look and smacked my lips. "Girl, you and I both know I have so much work to do at Black Lush, and I told you, the last person I should be getting close to is him. Shit can go all the way sideways."

But you already know you can't avoid him. You have to enter the next phase of your plan.

I'd worked as a talent liaison for Black Lush Adult Entertainment Agency for years, but I only did contract jobs for them now. I just couldn't tell Des that because it was my other business that was making me busier than ever. Not to mention the other shit that gave me nightmares just thinking about it.

Destiny was quiet for a minute before nodding. "Even not knowing the entire story, I understand that shit could hit the fan. If I'm being honest, I'm not sure this is a good idea either."

"I had a feeling you were nervous for me," I told her, her honesty surprisingly putting me more at ease.

"I am. But, Genesis, you're the toughest woman I know, and my gut is telling me that you're in more trouble than you're letting on and the only person who can help you is him."

I didn't respond because my mind was all over the place, which was so unlike me. That was the crazy thing about being in love with a man you were wrong for in every way. Pharaoh was a boss. A man who half the city respected, the other half feared. I was no good for him. I'd known it the first day I met it.

Yet, how to do you tell a man who was used to women falling at his feet that you were the one woman who could be his downfall if either of you gave into the all-consuming feelings that were impossible to ignore whenever you were in the same room together?

CHAPTER 4

Fuck Bitches, Get Pussy

wo weeks later …

PHAROAH

When I was in my early twenties, I messed around with a woman I hadn't known was in a forty-year marriage. She told me she was widow, but her husband approached me at a strip club I hadn't even thought about acquiring at the time.

He was drunk off his ass and had asked me point blank if I was fucking his wife. I wasn't a liar, so I told him yeah. He wanted to pull some tough guy shit in the club, but he wasn't stupid. He thought he had the upper hand and would catch me weeks later when my defenses were down after I dropped off one of my kids to her mom's house.

His aim was good.

My reflexes were better.

As he was bleeding out, he started talking about all kinds of shit. Things that annoyed me because although I was in the wrong, he'd been abusing his wife and felt like he'd successfully manipulated her to never want anyone but him.

The last thing I expected him to ask me as he was dying was why I hadn't confronted him like a man and asked him to trade his wife for one of my women. I laughed at his goofy ass because women weren't meant to be traded and bargained like they were disposable and weren't human beings. My laughing got him heated again and he cursed me out, saying women would be my downfall because I put pussy on a pedestal.

He was right. I did. Always had, probably always would.

He was still chanting those words like a curse as he drew his last breath.

I wasn't superstitious, but to my knowledge, that had been the first married woman I fucked with, and it wasn't lost on me that I hadn't had a marriage last yet.

The thing was, I didn't just fall for females. I fell for pussy.

Tight pussy.

Well-worn pussy.

Old pussy.

Pretty pussy.

Pierced pussy.

Soft pussy.

Shaved pussy.

Hairy pussy.

I didn't discriminate, but I still had standards. Although I didn't put a price on my dick, many women did. Drug lord. Kingpin. Dope Boy. Didn't matter what they referred to me as, I ran shit, and everybody in the Chicago area knew I was that muthafucka and what I was worth.

Getting into the business, I was humble ... until I wasn't. My mind focused on building an empire across the Midwest before conquering the United States instead of focusing only on the city I loved. Women flocked to me without me even having to lift a finger, but I loved the chase, I just never got to do much chasing.

Without a good and loyal woman by our side, men wouldn't be shit. I'd seen as much when my mom passed away and my pops turned into the skeleton of himself, weeks away from losing his clout in the streets and his business to every enemy waiting to strike. I remember watching him deteriorate and being pissed that although I loved my mom and missed her, too, I was disappointed that my father let heartache overtake him so much that it was impossible for him to find himself once he was already lost.

So I did what I had to do. What I was born to do despite appearing like I was the last muthafucka in the family to take over.

I started running the Pierce family empire at ten years old under the ruse of my older brothers who weren't good for shit but being the face of the business and muscle. Back then, I didn't notice I was different than other kids my age. Not just because I was running a drug empire and was barely double digits, but because my mind worked differently than everyone else. I was smarter than I realized and could see a map of the city and understand precisely where we could sneak in extra shipments from Mexico and some countries overseas.

I could spot a weak government official from a mile away and know how to manipulate them to get on our payroll. I understood the weaknesses of our enemies and I trusted our partnerships and allies who had just as much to lose as we did.

I fucked up sometimes, but I was more successful at playing chess than our enemies who were trying to take the throne.

Chess was a game of logic and reasoning, and all you had were your wits and strategy as methods of influence. While most boys in my hood were playing basketball and football in hopes of landing a scholarship that would take their family out of poverty, I was entering chess tournaments to learn and develop skills that no one in my family or circle were capable of teaching.

That's where I met the Crownes.

I'd just won my thirtieth match, which had pissed me off because I wanted to win fifty before my eleventh birthday, but the streets never slept and therefore, neither did I.

Stan was the first to approach me. I knew who he was. Everybody in Chicago did. Stan the Man had gone pro until a career-ending injury took him out of the NBA for good. At the height of his career, he'd been dating Duchess and several other women, but it was at his lowest point—broke, bankrupt, and borderline suicidal—that Duchess saved him from himself when he lost count of how many friends, fans, and family turned their back on him. Duchess wasn't going to let Stan lose more of himself than he already did, so they sold all the shit Stan had, including two of his championship rings, and began investing in small businesses together, creating Crowne Enterprises. Then they got into restaurants and the wine and liquor business. From there, they dove into real estate and retail. At least that's the shit people knew about.

Stan and I hadn't talked long before he invited me over for dinner. Looking back, I was surprised I never thought to bring security with me, especially being a kid. However, I trusted him off the bat. At the Crowne Estate is where I met Duchess, a woman I'd only heard about through associates of my pops.

Duchess came from a crime family, while Stan came from a line of athletes. Both knew what wealth felt like, they just came about that shit differently. I knew within minutes of sitting down for dinner that their agenda wasn't one I saw coming.

Adoption. It was a word I'd never really thought about even though I'd ended up in foster care with my brothers when I was a toddler after my parents ran into some legal issues, but it was quickly resolved.

The thing was, my father was still living, and I had older brothers who could care for me, but Stan and Duchess had a way of presenting you with another life you never even knew you were looking for. After all, my father only had months to live at most. Duchess knew that. So did Stan. And unfortunately, so did our enemies as word got around.

When pops passed, the Crownes entered an alliance with my family, both my older brothers relieved to no longer be forced to be in a life they never wanted. They hadn't been built for this shit. Not like me.

I kept my last name for a while, but Pops had one last thing to tell me before he passed. "You will always be a Pierce, but a Pharoah needs a crown."

Not able to completely get rid of the name that belonged to the people who brought me into this world, I legally made my middle name Pierce the day I changed my last name.

Then the true work began.

Duchess knew the Crownes wouldn't rise to the top without getting their hands dirty, which was why they adopted me. There were no secrets between us back then. We all knew why I was a Crowne and I was okay with it. Nash was their only child they had when they met me. In a way, Nash was a lot like Stan. Clean. Put together. More heart than brutality. Whereas I was more like Duchess, the two of us bonding early on. She understood my grind. She appreciated my grit. Money and power were our motivations, but family and loyalty were the key to the success of the Crownes. Without people you can truly trust who were willing to give their life for yours, ruling a city was a pipe dream.

They weren't the family I needed since I still had mine, but they were the family I was missing. It felt like I finally had people who understood me and could teach me how to truly be king of the streets. Offer me protection from our enemies. Jock and I didn't find out about each other until we were in our twenties. He was the son my father never knew he had. *Ironic now that I think about it.* Our bond was instant, and over the years, he'd become the man I trusted most. My crew got a lot better with Jock around since he had this instinct when it came to people. What I lacked, he had.

Over thirty years later, Crowne Enterprises was involved with more legal and illegal business ventures than Stan ever thought possible, but Duchess had always known they were destined for greatness.

Funny thing was, I'm sure neither Stan nor Duchess thought that the day they adopted me, five years later, they'd be grandparents. Just like I never suspected that even though the kids I had with the woman I just got off the phone with were grown as hell, I would still allow her to curse my ass out.

Good reason, though, since Francine learned I'd plotted to kill her current man. An emotional decision I wasn't proud of that would hopefully be the last irrational thing I'd do since Genesis returned.

"Why you in this corner lookin' butt hurt?" Hollis teased, as him, Saint, and Jedidiah took seats next me in the VIP booth at Scarlet, my newest Chicago gentleman's lounge and probably the most important.

The club had actually been around for years, but after Saint and his crew, The Drifters, were hired to clean up a mass murder that sent the prior owner running for the hills, I'd taken over the business, changed the name, and transformed it from a cheap strip club known for dollar hoes giving free blows to a high-end establishment offering only the top tier in stripping, sex, and all the exclusive offerings in packages created by Jade.

There were three more opening in the States, and three around the world—different names, but each one just as special and part of a bigger, seven-layer plan that I hoped worked out like the Crownes and others needed it to.

"I'm not hurt," I told him, taking a sip of Clase Azul, the premium tequila that I always kept in stock. "I just can't stand bitch ass muthafuckas who finally get a taste of some good pussy, then act brand new. Can't believe my goddamn friend would be down for wifin' up my ex."

"You got too many fuckin' exes," Jedidiah pointed out. "You ain't get that shit at Nash and Jade's wedding? If niggas didn't wife up women to avoid steppin' on your toes, there wouldn't be any pussy left in Chicago."

I frowned, looking over my glass at Jedidiah. "Damn, JD. Korie really do got you out here actin' different. I liked it betta when yo' big ass ain't say shit."

"Tell a muthafucka the truth, and he tell you you

actin'different," Jedidiah mumbled, shaking his head before taking a swig of his beer.

"Are you still in love with Francine?" Saint asked.

"Hell nah."

"Didn't you give them your blessing when they started dating?"

I shrugged. "So what?"

"If you gave your blessing, why you try to kill homeboy's ass then?" Hollis asked.

"I wasn't gonna kill him. Just wanted the bullet to graze his ass a little."

Hollis frowned. "Nigga, you weren't tryin' to graze shit. You ain't pull a Glock on his ass. You brought out an AK-47 assault rifle."

I waved him off. "Whateva, man. I came to my senses before anything went down. Francine was my first wife, and even though we got a divorce, I'll always have her back," I explained.

"Bullshit," Saint spat. "You in yo' feelings because she's the first woman you ever truly loved, and had you not fucked around and cheated on her, you'd still be together."

"Instead, you went into a downward spiral of sleeping with nameless women to bury the agonizing pain you felt from losing the woman you knew you would fundamentally base every woman after her on," Jedidiah added. "It's a messy cycle, and until you forgive yourself for your infidelity, you'll never have the healthy relationship you secretly long for."

"Damn, preacher JD for the win!" Hollis exclaimed.

They weren't wrong about my misplaced anger, but they had the woman all wrong. Honestly, my mood lately ain't have shit to do with Francine getting married. I was actually happy for her. I'd been thrown off by Genesis' return, and although I'd seen Noble a few times in the past couple weeks, I'd taken great strides to avoid seeing her, which was fucked up. I didn't hide from women. *Except those stalker types I have restraining orders against, and that crazy chick who seemed to pop up in bushes in the most random places.*

I couldn't bring up Genesis though. My brothers didn't know about her outside of what they witnessed at the wedding and I wanted to keep it that way. I continued staring ahead, quiet for a bit as I let their words settle before I finally told them, "I never cheated on another woman after that."

"We know," Saint stated.

"Which, I gotta tell you, bruh, it's pretty impressive to have been with the women you have and not had that shit overlap," Hollis said. "Like, do you keep a chart or sumthin? Or maybe a spreadsheet? I don't even understand where you have the time to be with so many of 'em. Or do you have so many one-night stands that it balances out your week, and if you don't promise any of them a relationship, you ain't fuckin' up? A part of me thinks the only reason you ain't cheat is because some of your relationships only last a week."

"One of y'all shut him the fuck up," I pleaded, taking another swig of tequila.

"Why did you let him have his bachelor party here?" Saint asked, looking at Paul, Francine's fiancé.

"Ion know man. We been boys since the sandbox, so I felt kinda bad tryin' to shoot his ass when Francine and I been over for a minute." *Plus, I realized my actions ain't have shit to do with Francine.*

"And you've been married a couple times since then," Hollis chimed in.

"That too," I admitted. "I told his best man he could have the party here, but this shit had to be in the evening.

We got the whole place reserved for later tonight for some muthafuckas paying a lot more than they are."

"You still on your hiatus?" Jedidiah asked.

"Sort of, but I don't understand how you did this shit before Korie, man. I'm horny as a muthafucka."

"Wait, you weren't playin' when you told Jackie D you weren't gonna have sex for a while?" Hollis asked. "Why the fuck would you do that? You have the healthiest sex life out of all of us." He took a sip of his drink and mumbled, "More kids, too."

"Shit is too hot in Chicago right now and I need to be as alert as possible," I explained, ignoring Hollis' joke that they all rotated on telling too damn much. "I'm not holding myself to it, but the Velvet app just launched and I gotta prepare for my trip to Tulum, Mexico to talk to Constantine."

"I should prolly go with you," Hollis suggested. "Gotta make sure the app is working properly before you present everything."

"Bet. I'll text you my flight info." Motion on the side of the club got my attention, my brothers and I all turning our heads and touching our pistols.

"Tommy just knocked over a few glasses," Saint stated.

Tommy began cursing as he picked up the broken pieces.

"That's coming out your paycheck!" Hollis yelled, to which I just shook my damn head. He ain't control shit in this place, so Tommy was good.

"It's shit like that that lets me know something's coming," I told them. "Broken glass. A bird that got caught in the grill of my car today. Shit happens in threes." I wasn't superstitious, but I believed in signs. "And after everything that went down with Igor and his crew, the Russians have been too damn quiet."

"Some of my contacts tell me more have arrived in Chicago and were spotted in Skokie and Rogers Park, but they're keeping a low profile," Saint mentioned. "Probably getting more intel first, and we have more than a few frenemies who will sing like canaries when threatened."

"One of my guys mentioned Igor's son may be here, too," I added.

"Shit," Hollis huffed. "We pop off one Popov just to have to deal with a younger, more egotistical version."

"We ain't even sure you popped off anybody," I told him. "Yo' ass almost gave Duchess a heart attack."

Hollis pretended to laugh, and then straightened up his face. "We agreed never to talk about that lapse in judgement."

"I ain't promise shit."

"Not your finest moment," Saint added.

Jedidiah shrugged. "I always knew you were a little bitch when it came to blood, so ain't mean shit to me."

"Bruh, I can handle blood," Hollis defended. "But that shit was gushing everywhere. I swear some of it was coming out that one dude's eyeball. And his eyes turned purple, which reminded me of grapes. Y'all know I love grapes."

"I don't see how you can eat so many frozen grapes," I said, laughing at his ass.

"It's a delicacy that's too exquisite for your palate." He pretended to pop some imaginary grapes in his mouth. "Anyway, that place looked like a warzone."

Jedidiah nodded. "'Cause it was. We knew if that night ended in a bloodbath, there would be consequences. Igor wasn't as bad as some of the other Russian territory leaders, so best believe they are plotting and planning their retaliation when they think our guard is down." He looked to me. "The easiest way for Russians who aren't familiar with Chicago to infiltrate our city and get close to us is through drug trafficking. We gotta set up a meeting with your guys and mine to make sure we're ready."

"Agreed," I told him. "Let's set something up this week. Igor's son hasn't been in much media, so we're working on getting more intel."

"I'll see what I can find, too," Hollis added. You wouldn't know it by the way he acted, but Hollis was one of the best hackers around.

I glanced at my 18K gold Audemars Piguet Royal Oak watch, wondering if any of my brothers noticed I only wore it on days when I knew I'd be stressed the fuck out, but needed to keep myself in check. "This bachelor party should be wrapping up soon, and Genesis asked me to stop by to discuss some things about Noble."

"Wait, you got the results?" Saint asked.

"Yep." I downed the rest of my tequila, pissed that I was looking forward to seeing Genesis. "Noble is my son and we've been getting to know each other. He's pretty damn smart, too. I'll introduce him to the family soon."

"Looking forward to it," Hollis stated, smirking. He wanted to tease my ass about having eleven kids, but I also knew Hollis was a great uncle to them, even if he did annoy the shit out of me.

Damn. I didn't have eleven kids now.

I had twelve.

I needed to remember that shit.

And I definitely didn't want to tell them that Noble was out of town with some friends, because no doubt, jokes about me and Genesis would have kicked off. Until now, they hadn't teased me about her that much.

Better yet, maybe having them roast my ass would help me keep my dick in my pants this time.

CHAPTER 5

Fuck Caution, Be Reckless

GENESIS

"This is a bad idea," I muttered into the phone as I changed my outfit for a third time, settling on lounge pants and a top so it didn't seem like I was trying too hard to look cute.

"No, it's not," Destiny, said rolling her eyes at me through our FaceTime call. "Didn't we already talk about this while I was there? Y'all need to have a grown folks conversation without Noble being there. Plus, you need to ask him whatever it is that you failed to ask him last time because you were too busy sucking his dick."

I frowned. "You ain't right."

"Where is the lie though?"

I rolled my eyes before glancing around the suite. "Yeah, well, inviting him to a hotel room hardly seems like a good idea. He's gonna ask me why a hotel and not my condo."

"And you're going to tell him that you're getting some construction done on your place like we discussed," she reminded.

"I guess that's better than admitting I don't want him to know where I live. Which probably means I shouldn't be seeing him at all, especially without Noble."

"You worry too damn much! I saw the way he looked at you at that wedding, and he's already proving Noble is important to him, even before the DNA results came through. So he's gonna be in your life regardless. Maybe try and not overthink tonight. You've met with men like him before, and in this case, y'all have a short history."

"A short, *complicated* history," I reminded.

"Doesn't matter. Better short and complicated than long and messy."

"Did you decide to come into town for your cousin's baby shower in a couple months?" I asked, changing the subject. Destiny was from a small town in Illinois that was about two hours from downtown, but she hated staying with her family when visited.

"Probably. If so, you already know I'll be staying at your place whether you're in town or not."

"That's cool." The knock at the door forced me to take a deep breath. "He's finally here."

"Oh shit! Okay, girl, call me tomorrow."

"Will do."

For those brief seconds after Destiny disconnected our call and I walked to the door to let Pharaoh in, I took several deep breaths, trying my best to calm my nerves.

My eyes widened at the sight of a large, burly man standing a few feet away, until I realized it was Jock.

"Don't mind him," Pharaoh stated. "Jock will wait out in the hallway while we talk."

Jock gave me a quick head nod that I returned.

"No problem." I closed the door, my breath catching when instead of walking completely inside of the suite, Pharaoh stopped right in front of me, his sexy scent wafting through my nostrils.

Damn, why does he always smell so delicious? There was nothing sexier to me than a man who smelled good and Pharaoh *always* smelled good.

And he'd come tonight despite his apprehension. I wasn't even sure if he still frequented The Drake Hotel, but from what I remembered, there were only certain places Pharaoh did business and The Drake Hotel was one of them. The historic hotel had been around since the 1920s and supplied quick access to Chicago's Gold Coast neighborhood and The Magnificent Mile. On the outside, it seemed like only those of high-society, politicians, and tourists looking for a taste of Chicago history stayed here. What they didn't tell you was that The Drake Hotel was a criminal's sanctuary. If you didn't know what went down here, you probably shouldn't be doing whatever the hell you did.

"I hope you invited me here tonight to give me some answers."

I swallowed back my attraction. "I did."

The way he looked back at me hinted that I wouldn't have wanted to know what he'd do if I didn't. Probably something sexual. *Or is that wishful thinking?*

He finally walked farther into my suite, surveying the room in a way that to most would seem like a simple observance, but to me, I noticed the slight crease in his forehead as he took everything in, trying to spot any obvious differences from the style I was sure he had memorized from other meetings he'd attended here.

His eyes grazed over the windows and number of vantage points someone could have from the office building across the street, before settling on the slightly crooked painting that I'd accidentally bumped when I checked into the room.

"I ran into it earlier," I explained when he observed it a second too long.

"I know." He glanced down. "You sat in the chair and took off your heels, slightly bending to rub your feet, but it was too dark in the room, so you cut on the lamp." He angled his head. "When it didn't turn on, you realized it wasn't plugged in and you moved the nightstand to do so, which caused you to angle your body to reach the plug. When you stood, your shoulder tapped the painting."

"Uh, exactly …" My mouth slightly parted at the reminder that when it came to small details, Pharaoh was one of the best.

He looks so damn good when he gets all perceptive, too. Even when he wasn't trying, I still had to keep myself in check around him. Tonight, he was wearing a black tee, black jeans, and all black Jordans. However, it was the way half his dreads were tied while the rest flowed freely, giving me a better view of his almost onyx eyes, and the way his tongue slipped out to moisten his lips that made it extra difficult to focus on the task at hand.

"You're late," I finally mentioned. "And you're never late."

"I had shit to do," he said. "Business doesn't stop because you suddenly want to talk after a couple weeks of silence."

He kept me waiting on purpose. This was booty call hours

and he damn well knew it. “I haven’t been radio silent. We’ve discussed Noble.”

He laughed. “Genesis, I ain’t got the patience for your games tonight, and I gotta get back to Scarlet.”

“I’m not on games tonight.”

“Hmm.” His eyes roamed over my loose pants and tank that I’d purposely worn since a dress would force me to spend the night clenching my thighs together. “Not sure why you’re wearing pants.”

I placed a hand on my hip. “And how did you suppose I greet you at the door?”

He rubbed the bottom of his chin, eyeing my every move. “You already know how I feel about you in too many damn clothes. And if you ain’t ready to confess what I want to know, then I guess there’s only one other way you can keep my mouth occupied and my mind on other shit.”

I swallowed. “There won’t be any of that.” *Really though, sis?* I was a ball of nerves wrapped in a hot mess. The way he smirked proved neither of us believed the shit I was talking.

“Are you hungry?” I asked, my voice sounding more breathless than I would have liked. I needed a distraction to gather my thoughts and food would be a great one.

“Yeah, take off your pants and get on the bed,” he whispered, his words sending a chill down my spine and catching me so off guard, I almost stumbled.

“For what?”

“So I can eat.”

“But I cooked dinner,” I muttered, ignoring him as I stepped away and began taking out glass containers of food. I figured that would be the moment he asked why we hadn’t met at my place since I obviously packed up food I’d cooked earlier. I was sure Noble had mentioned something to him about my condo, but he always met up with

Noble, and a man like Pharaoh had to know I was avoiding having him at my house.

However, his next words weren't that at all.

"I ain't expect you to cook shit," he noted. "What I planned to eat been ready for me."

Oh fuck. This was a bad fucking idea. I'd known it the moment I requested he come to my hotel room.

"That's not why I asked you here," I semi-lied, knowing damn well I had hoped the night would end up in bed regardless of how badly I needed to talk to him about more important matters.

"But I'm here now." He took two long strides toward me, his breath teasing my neck. "You can go to sleep frustrated or with my tongue between your legs. The choice is yours."

I shivered as I thought about his tongue. A mouth I hadn't had please me in too damn long. I wasn't an angel in the bedroom, and I'd been with men after him. Yet, there was something about how Pharaoh did it that made all others seem like boys trying to take care of a man's job.

"You can't tell me yo' pussy don't miss how the fuck my tongue used to do it," he murmured, his lips grazing my earlobe.

"Fuck you," I whispered, because he knew I missed it. Oral sex had kind of been our thing back in the day, and it was because of him that I knew all tongues weren't created equal.

So many women ran into the Tough Tongue Tommy type. The kind of man who was too rough with the pressure he applied to her clit, assuming he wanted her to ring it like an unanswered doorbell. Typically, those Tommy types liked to look at you with the creepy, unblinking eyes and make all kind of weird groaning noises.

Then there were the Too Eager Cleavers. God forbid a

woman who was already apprehensive about oral sex meet a man who seemed patient and experienced, only to realize he's too damn enthusiastic, licking it with too much spit and not enough technique. Disappointment at its finest that usually resulted in wet ass saliva sheets and no orgasm.

Before Pharaoh, I thought I liked the Directionally Challenged Davids. A David asked how you wanted him to pleasure your clit, so you got exactly what you wanted. To me, directing him was better than finding out he was a Tommy or Cleaver.

It wasn't until Pharaoh introduced me to a whole other kind of man that I realized how much stimulation I'd been lacking in my life. In a way, it was because of how he moved his tongue, his mouth, the way he commanded that I sit on his face that had me realizing early on that nothing would compare to the thrill I got when I eased my pussy down over The Throne of a Pharaoh. My favorite kind of man.

He knew how to please me when I wasn't even sure what I needed. Commanded me when, with any other man, I'd curse his ass out.

My hands had a mind of their own as I pushed my pants down my legs, going for the panties next, until he grabbed my arm and led me to the bed. I gracefully crawled to the spot I thought he wanted me, but his voice rumbled in the room with a concise, "Stop fuckin' moving."

I froze on all fours and turned to look at him, gasping when I felt his tongue lick my ass cheek as he began pulling down my panties with his teeth.

My eyes were wide the fuck open as he knelt at the bed, grabbed both my ankles, and pulled me to the edge. To have a tall, strong man like Pharaoh get on his knees and spread my legs open with a lustful, yet predatory, look was almost too much to handle.

Running a long finger up and down my pussy, his eyes sparked as I grew wetter with every touch. He pushed my legs even farther and inhaled before he slipped a finger inside of me, causing me to slightly buck off the bed.

"Hold still," he demanded.

Seriously? I tried my best not to move as his fingers gently twisted inside of my pussy as he found my G-spot and continued to move in slow strokes. I wanted to scream from pleasure or bite a pillow, but I was already having a hard time staying still, Pharaoh popping my pussy any time I disobeyed.

I was close to the brink when he removed his fingers. Glancing down at him, I opened my mouth to ask why he'd stopped, but shut it the moment I noticed the serious expression on his face.

"Sit up," he commanded, to which I readily obeyed. "Squat down," he followed, which was difficult as hell to do on the bed when my feet couldn't get a good grip on the plush mattress.

"You must not want this tongue," he taunted.

I do. I do. When I finally succeeded at maintaining my balance, he slipped his head between my legs, causing my entire body to shiver at the sight of him seated on the floor with his head in between my legs.

"Now ease the fuck down and do that shit slow," he ordered.

My breathing was labored, and my thighs quivered as I got closer to his mouth, refusing to tremble. I only had one thought on my mind as I felt the first brush of his deliciously dominating tongue.

The queen has now taken over the throne.

And I rode that thang like I hadn't had a man lick my

pussy since we'd been together fifteen years ago, and in a way, it wasn't entirely untrue. No one was even worth an honorable mention when experiencing a tongue like his.

I felt his shit all the way to my soul, grateful when he gripped my thighs and dipped his tongue even deeper before kneading my clit, a second orgasm quickly sending me over the edge of no return to the point where I saw stars before everything went black.

It took me a while to wake up, only to find Pharaoh sitting patiently at the desk, watching me … waiting. My pussy still on full display for him.

"Damn, you didn't even put a sheet over me?"

He shook his head. "Nope."

I observed how chill he was. "Do you want me to return the favor?"

"I'm good," he stated, his expression unreadable. "I hate waiting, but I only did since I'm the reason you needed the rest."

"How long did I doze off?"

"You always fall asleep for twenty minutes after you orgasm."

I gave a sheepish grin, unable to deny his claim.

The moment should feel awkward, but that was another thing I liked about the person I was around Pharaoh. Anything we did—no matter how wild and vulnerable it was—I never felt weird after, just nervous.

Clearing my throat, I grabbed the cotton robe I draped over the chair earlier and walked over to the food I'd forgotten about.

"I got something for you," I told him, as I tried to get my bearings and shake off what just happened.

"Besides what you just gave me?"

I nodded and lifted the bottle of Patrón Silver out of the ice bucket. He mentioned in a conversation years ago that it was one of his go-to liquors if someone wanted to discuss business with him after he'd already had a long day.

He thanked me before putting some ice in a couple glasses, opening the bottle, and pouring us both a double shot.

"Oh, I don't need any," I told him.

"You must be about to tell me some shit I'm not gonna like since you brought this." He pointed to the bottle before handing me my glass. "And you seem too damn tense for a woman who just had two orgasms, so I think you should drink this for your nerves."

I took a sip of the liquor, hoping it worked it's magic fast since I really was relaxed after what we'd just done. I was just anxious to ask him the question I'd been meaning to ask since I returned.

"Okay, I guess I'll just get right to it because I know you want answers." I took another quick sip, savoring the small jolt it sent through my body. "I want to talk a little about Noble, but that's not the only reason I asked you here tonight or why I came back in town."

He smirked. "I figured as much."

My fingers played with the rim of the glass as I wondered why he was being so calm—and giving me the best orgasm I'd had since … him—considering just a couple weeks ago, he'd been cursing my ass out for coming back into his life unannounced and springing Noble on him. "So, I know what I'm about to ask you may come as a huge shock, but I hope that you hear me out."

He raised a curious eyebrow at me, watching me over his glass as he took another sip of Patrón. "I'm listening."

"I want to work with you," I blurted.

The look on his face was a cross between amusement and disbelief. "You do, huh? You worked for me before and you see how that turned out?"

I frowned. "Work with you, not for you. I know it didn't work out last time, but—"

"Shit was good until you decided to go without even calling, messaging, or even sending a damn postcard from where you ended up."

"I had my reasons," I told him.

"Which I'm still waiting to hear."

I sighed. "Let's not act like our situation was normal. Like you didn't know something was off or that you even cared about me when we first met."

"When we first met, you were a stripper looking for employment at the first gentlemen's club I owned. A vibrant beauty with the seductive face of every man's filthy fantasy, and an ass so round and perfect, I could have sworn it was fake until I cupped it in my hands."

"I should have told you who I was right away."

"You should have handled a lot of shit differently," he said. "It wasn't just on you though. I fucked up letting you get too close."

His words stung, although they shouldn't. "Twenty-seven-year-old Genesis had a chip on her shoulder and too much to lose," I confessed. "At forty-two, life shifts to give you more perspective on what's important and what isn't." Taking a deep breath, I admitted, "Which is why I want us to team up."

"No," he stated. "Seeing each other outside of discussing Noble is out of the question."

My lips parted. "I thought you agreed to hear me out? How can you go down on me like that, then play me as soon as I start talking?"

"Me play you?" he repeated, shaking his head.

"You didn't even let me tell you my proposition."

"Okay, what is it?" His question was simple, but something about the look in his eyes gave me pause. "What? You ain't got shit to say anymore?"

"I won't let you talk to me any kind of way," I warned. "But you should know that the McKays are now allies with Ronan's crew."

"The Crownes are good with the Irish, and I don't give a shit what the McKays do, especially Eric McKay. His offspring owe me their firstborn kids with all the outstanding favors he has yet to return."

"But they are still your allies, right?" He didn't answer, so I continued, assuming I was right. "I figured you wouldn't care, and I thought it was useless information when I heard about it. Except, now I'm not so sure."

I walked over to my bag and pulled out a file folder of photos. "I had someone take these and wasn't surprised to see Ronan and Eric chatting it up, but it was who they were talking to that gave me pause."

"Is this …"

"Boris Popov, Igor Popov's son? Yeah, it is."

He tried to remain expressionless, but only someone who had observed him like I had all those years ago knew when he was pleasantly surprised with the information.

"I want in," I told him. "I know you, Pharaoh, and I heard about what went down with the Russians. This may look like a simple conversation—"

"But it isn't," he finished, taking a second look at the last close-up of the men shaking hands. "Can I keep these?"

"As long as you consider letting me work with you to bring Boris down," I told him. "You don't have to tell your family I'm involved, and we'll be discreet. An enemy of my enemy is my friend, and if you let me, I can be an asset."

He only held my eyes briefly before standing and

surprising me by kissing me on the cheek. "Let me think about it."

"Wait!" I stood from my chair. "You're leaving just like that?"

He stopped when he was almost to the door and turned, his face unreadable when he asked, "What the fuck are we doing here, Ginx?"

"We're trying to find some common ground. I get you have to think about it, but just know that—"

"You never told me who the fuck you were until I was already in too deep," he interrupted, his eyes looking slightly pained when he said it, but he masked it. "I was hypnotized by this feisty vixen who was unlike any woman I'd met, not knowing who the fuck she really was."

"I fell for you just as hard," I admitted, my voice cracking, which pissed me off since this was not the moment for raw emotion. "If anyone can understand the situation I was in, it should be you." My eyes darted across his. "You want to know why I left, but you already know the answer, don't you?"

"I told you I'd take care of you," he said, his fists tightening at his side. "I promised you that if you were honest with me, I'd take care of you."

"Honest? Like I was the only one lying!" I placed my hands on my hips. "How long did it take for you to realize I was Booker's sister?"

"Not long," he confessed, stepping closer to me, my eyes on his chest, refusing to look up at his face. "You and I both know we had a deeper connection, though. We fooled around, but it wasn't about the sex. We didn't even cross that line until much later." Placing two fingers under my chin, he lifted my face so I had no choice but to get lost in his unapologetic eyes. "It wasn't until my dick was buried balls deep in your pussy, my body on the road to ecstasy, that I noticed a guilt in your eyes that I'd never seen before. Here I was, looking into the eyes of the woman I loved, and she had me so wrapped around her goddamn finger that I'd missed the signs."

I released a forced laugh. "It was over before it even started," I told him, straightening my face, anger replacing the elation I'd felt earlier. "Because at the end of the day, you killed my brother. The person I loved most in this world. A man who had fallen victim to the streets, but had a good heart. On top of that, you never told me you killed him."

"I'm not sorry for killing Booker because there was no world in which both of us could co-exist," he admitted. "But I am sorry you lost your brother. The Brooks family had been enemies of the Pierce family for decades, but I was willing to drop that shit when I became a Crowne. It was your brother who said it was either him or me. The streets couldn't have two kings."

"You forget how well I got to know you," I huffed. "You're logical and rational. Yeah, you can be cruel as hell, but if you have to kill someone, you take your time creating a plan of action first."

"He came for my throne."

"You came for his just as hard!" I exclaimed. "There are two sides to every story."

"And a truth as fucked up as the fact that from day one, you lied to me and you know how I feel about liars."

"If I hadn't lied, you would have killed me on the spot. Do you think I wanted to work for my family? Losing Booker gave me no choice. I hated the situation I was in," I confessed. "It felt like I'd lose no matter what I did. Either avenge Booker and my family or lose the man I fell in love with."

"Or trust that man to figure some shit out."

"Which would probably include me disowning my family," I pointed out. "A mother I would do anything for a father who is the best man I know."

The vein in his neck popped. "Instead, you were willing to pretend to be a stripper, get close to me, and slit the throat of the man you had just fucked for a brother who was already dead."

I slapped him across the face, but his head barely moved at the motion. "I never want to hear you talk about my brother that way. Especially when I didn't go through with it. I lost everything that night I decided to leave Chicago."

"We both lost," he stated.

"No, we didn't," I corrected. "You may feel like you lost me, but I didn't just lose the man I love. I lost my family anyway since even though I see them, I couldn't be close to them." I stood taller and kept my face firm. "Or did you forget when you called the hit on me?"

His eyes searched mine. "I caught you standing over me with a knife to my throat and a needle of some kind of toxin in the other hand."

"And I didn't do it."

"I couldn't chance it. And I lost time with my son," he added. "A son you failed to tell me about until a couple weeks ago. A son who not only looks like me, but has my mannerisms and intelligence. A Crowne and Pierce if I ever saw one."

"Noble will always be a part of me too," I corrected. "And I'd like to think you wouldn't kill your own son despite how much you hate my family."

"I didn't touch your family after you left Chicago," he interjected. "Your mother and I even worked together on one occasion, and she never mentioned Noble either."

"I made her promise not to." *Amongst other secrets.*

"Which brings me to the other reason I want to work together to bring down Boris Popov." My heart was racing and my emotions were high.

"Which is?" he asked.

"My mother, Esi. She's Ghanaian, but before she moved to the United States, she lived in the UK and worked for foreign intelligence." I took a deep breath, trying to keep my emotions in check before I revealed, "She's been missing for six months. My father thought she was in the UK on some secret mission that she can't disclose, but that's not the case. I think Boris Popov killed her. I believe my dad suspected it, too, because he passed away two months ago."

"Shit." Pharaoh placed both hands on the chair in front of him. "So your dad isn't alive like you claimed at my brother's wedding?"

I shook my head. "He isn't."

"I didn't know since your family moved out of the city soon after you left." He stepped forward, then stopped himself, and I wondered if he was battling between wanting to comfort me, but knowing neither of us had ever been the hugging type when our emotions were already heightened. "Are you okay?"

"Hardly," I said honestly, walking into his outstretched arms, grateful he finally offered a hug. "But I will be … once I kill Boris." Even then I wasn't sure if I'd be okay, I'd be a helluva lot happier with him dead.

I could wait to analyze how *perfect* it felt hugging Pharaoh later.

CHAPTER 6

Fuck Coincidences, Know Thy Enemy

PHARAOH

"How the fuck did this happen?" I asked Keon, looking down at the bodies of four of my best guys, keeping my anger in check. I had to when no doubt, others who worked for me would be rattled when they heard about this.

"Cash and Jock are tryin' to figure that shit out now, but the security cameras were disconnected."

Most on my level had stash houses, but I had tired of that shit early on in the game. I preferred hideaway mansions. The kind of places you'd find in the richest neighborhoods in the city. I never kept drugs or money in the mansions long, but on shipment days, business was booming, and I had my employees on a schedule. I had a few mansions that were hard to find, and my Highland Park location was in a part of the suburbs that sat between two large hilltops and was surrounded by greenery.

"What about the cameras we had installed in the neighbor's yard?"

"Dead end," Jock said, stepping into the dining room. "He said he didn't even know the power went out in the middle of the night until him and his wife woke up and noticed the clocks needed to be reset."

"Then no one heard anything?"

"Doesn't seem like it," Cash answered. "The neighborhood feature on the Ring device that everyone is using doesn't say shit about a disturbance here either."

"Were Troy and Dex accounted for last night?"

Keon nodded. "Cash and I were with them most the night handling business. They may be snitches, but they punk asses couldn't pull of something like this."

"And they don't even know this place exists," Cash added.

I bent down, observing the way some of the bodies had been dismembered. "The twins put up a fight, so whoever did this made them die slowly."

"Not surprised," Cash stated. "Jake and Jeremy were two of our best fighters. There's no way there weren't at least seven guys who took them down."

I glanced back at Jock. "You good?"

"Yeah," he stated, cracking his knuckles. "Just wish I would have been here."

When I on boarded Jake and Jeremy, they had just been selling dope on the corners within a two-mile radius. They hadn't even been thinking big, but I saw their potential. Jock was the one to show them the ropes and had taken them under his wing. They were good guys who were loyal and had integrity, two qualities that were hard to find in drug dealers these days.

"I'll personally talk to Jake's wife and kids and make sure they know they have our financial support and sincerest condolences," I announced. "And last I heard, Jeremy was dating someone new, right?"

"He got back with his childhood sweetheart," Jock answered. "They were getting pretty serious again. I have her information."

I nodded. "We'll visit her as well."

I hated making visits like this, but if my men and women put their lives in danger for my business, the least I could do was make sure their families were taken care of if shit went left.

A chime indicated that someone had crossed the property line at the gate. "It's the Drifters," I mentioned, noticing the van from the window. Three minutes later, Saint and his cleanup crew arrived, most of his men dabbing fists with Cash and Keon upon arrival.

In addition to working for me, Cash and Keon were also a part of The Drifters. On one hand, Saint and I hadn't wanted them to run themselves thin. On the other, it was nice to have men we trusted working for both of us.

"Shit, not Jake and Jeremy," Saint stated after we greeted each other and stepped off into the foyer while Saint's crew got to work.

"I know. Jock and I are headed to tell their family."

"Who did it?"

I shrugged. "We're still trying to figure that shit out, but they didn't steal any drugs or money. We keep that shit pretty tightly sealed, but still."

"I agree," he said. "That shit don't make sense."

"It sho' the fuck don't." I glanced around to make sure none of the men were in earshot. "I think it was the Russians trying to leave a message."

"They've stayed quiet for this long," Saint retorted. "Why break in here and kill your men without taking any drugs or money?"

"To prove they can have close access to me if they wanted to," I speculated. "One of my contacts was able to get me a photo of Boris, Igor's son." I took out my phone and scrolled to the image I'd taken of photos Genesis gave me.

"Is that Ronan and Eric?"

I nodded. "Yeah, it's those fuckas. I was gonna call a family meeting at the estate today and got side-tracked by the break-in. I'll message the fam to meet tomorrow. We gotta figure this shit out fast. I don't want to lose anymore men because of unfinished Crowne business."

"This may not have been done by them," Saint reasoned. "We can't act until we have concrete facts." He squinted, observing me closely. "You usually don't want to do anything irrational without having all the intel anyway. What gives?"

"Nothing," I answered, keeping my mouth shut as I realized how badly I wanted it to be the Russians who killed my men. I didn't like looking over my shoulder, waiting for the enemy to strike. Especially after spending the other night holding Genesis in a moment of vulnerability after telling me that same enemy may have killed her mother.

* * *

TALKING to Jake and Jeremy's family had been tough. I even noticed Jock struggling to compose himself when Jake's wife broke down.

I'd had that talk with families before, but the shit never got easier. In a way, hella shit that used to not affect me took a toll every now and then.

After my talk with Saint, we agreed to call a family meeting tonight instead of the morning, except for Jade and Nash who were still on their extended honeymoon.

"Getting these photos helped," Hollis stated, pulling up a blown-up image of Boris on the large monitor, along with photos of several other men.

"I haven't seen some of these faces in years," Duchess stated, walking up to the monitor. After the wedding, Duchess and Stan went out of town, neither telling us that they traveled to Russia.

Jackie D was the only one who knew, which hadn't sat well with me when I found out a few hours ago. In the past, this was something I would have known before the others, which made me feel like there was something I was missing.

"I'm not surprised about Boris," Duchess stated, "but when Stan and I were overseas, our Russian contacts told us the Moscow Popovs had been attacked and most of the family was killed. However, I recognize some of them as the sons of Igor's cousins and Natasha's brothers."

"Why were they attacked?" Keaton asked.

"Battle of power," Duchess explained. "They haven't been too happy with the Popovs, and with Igor gone here in the States, their Russian frenemies decided to take action in Moscow."

"So basically we did them a favor?" Korie asked.

"Not exactly." Stan pointed to the screen. "By eliminating Igor and Natasha, we caused a domino effect, but from our understanding, the next family in line for the Bratva will be setting up house in Chicago soon. Boris doesn't have the support of the other Russian families."

"So this group has gone rogue," I declared. "Meaning we ain't dealing with the return of the Bratva to Chicago who we can build a new alliance with. We're dealing with exactly what we feared … organized Russian crime experts with a vendetta against the Crownes, my team in particular."

"We all have your back," Jedidiah encouraged. "You ain't in this shit alone, bruh."

"Appreciate it, but it's not me I'm worried about. It's everyone who works for me out there on these streets with no protection. Rogue or not, with Boris here, he doesn't just want revenge. He wants Igor's drug territories back, and I don't want to wake up every day to new bodies."

The room grew quiet, which only happened in my family when no one knew what to say about a situation that was out of our hands.

"We always prevail," Duchess fortified, her eyes solely on me. "I know today was rough for you, but those photos you got were good intel, and because of that, Hollis was able to locate the others hiding in our city."

"Maybe you should postpone Mexico," Queenie said, rolling her wheelchair into the room, briefly smiling at Jedidiah and Korie like they shared some kind of secret before focusing on me.

That was weird.

"It's not safe right now and the family should all be together," she stated.

"I understand," I told her. "But we all know how crucial the Velvet app is to our overall operation to expose the main underground human trafficking organization who's been responsible for a thirty percent increase in cases over the past few years. We did a soft launch, but all the contacts Jedidiah was able to get from Kevin Williams were already awaiting the official launch of the app. Setting things up in Mexico is a huge step. Igor gone or not, human trafficking is still at an all-time high, and through Hollis' findings, we know Natasha was a piece of that puzzle."

"And Carla Jean," Korie added, disdain in her voice. "She may have been a human trafficking victim herself, but her name came up in those sex trading files as a leader, not a victim. She turned out to be the kind of woman who would rather sell out her own daughter to the very people who made her life hell in order to secure funding for her venture capitalist firm. How many young women did she lure to trust her?"

Jedidiah pulled Korie to him as she spoke with such pain about the recent discovery that Carla Jean had known Tristan was going to be targeted that night she was killed and even supported it, doing nothing to save her daughter.

My eyes went to Creed who was standing in the corner showing little emotion. The usual during every family meeting since he lost his wife. It couldn't have been easy grieving, while watching your brothers fall in love around you. Especially with women who were close or connected to Tristan in some way.

"In due time, we'll find Carla Jean," Duchess stated, mainly to Korie.

"And I'll kill her myself," Creed vowed. "Slowly. *Painfully*. Without remorse." His voice was firm and laced with a certain viciousness I wasn't used to hearing from him. A man broken and out for revenge, biding his time until he could strike.

"A snake can only hide in the grass for so long before it has to search for something to eat," Duchess cited. "I'm disgusted that I ever called that woman a friend back in the day. Mark my words, she won't get away with it."

My thoughts drifted to Genesis, unable to stop my mind from realizing the correlation in Duchess' words. She and I shared a complicated past, and I wasn't dumb enough to continue trying to convince myself that I wanted to help her. Yet, I couldn't help but wonder if she was the snake, or the prey in the grass waiting to be eaten. Maybe a little of both? Could be neither.

"You're right, Pharaoh," Duchess stated, interrupting my thoughts. "You and Hollis will go to Mexico as planned, and Jedidiah and his team will back up yours here in Chicago."

I nodded, having already worked the details out with Jackie D, but still feeling the weight of my employees' safety on my shoulders.

After we wrapped everything up, Duchess asked me to stay behind. "You're upset with me," she mentioned as a statement rather than a question once everyone cleared the room except Stan.

"Not upset. Just wondering why I wasn't in the loop about Russia."

"With the return of Genesis, and the discovery of your son, you have enough on your plate."

I wasn't surprised she brought her up. What went down at the wedding may not have seemed like a big deal to everyone present, my siblings included. However, Duchess and Stan knew differently.

"How are you coping with her return?" Stan asked.

I shrugged. "I'm cool. Just trying to get to know Noble. I'll introduce him to the family after this mess with the Russians settles."

Duchess smiled. "We'd like that, but I don't believe for one second that you're not affected by her return."

"She won't cloud my judgement," I stated.

"Her brother was the first man you ever killed," she said, her voice softer than before. "People don't just forget something like that, and in your case, you fell in love with that man's sister."

"True, but that was so many years ago."

"But it feels like yesterday," Stan speculated.

"I don't know about all that," I lied.

"You don't have to tell your family I'm involved, and we'll be discreet." Her words that night in her hotel room came rushing back. Even though I had a lot going on, there was so much that wasn't sitting right about the recent course of events. I was missing something big. I felt that shit in my soul.

I just hoped that when I figured it out, it wouldn't force me into a situation where I had to question my family. They knew me better than most, and I knew when they were keeping secrets from me. Mind made up, I planted the seed.

"We actually saw each other the other day because she'll be in Chicago for a while and wants to try and work on the same team instead of the opposite team this time."

Duchess and Stan shared a look. It was brief, but long enough for me to catch it.

"Are you sure that's a good idea?" Duchess asked.

"It's not," I admitted. "That's why I told her no."

"Good," Stan responded. "Maybe keep your relationship about Noble. We've made peace with the Brooks family, but you can never be too careful around someone who tried to kill you."

"Exactly."

Even as they switched topics, my mind was still reeling as I observed Duchess and Stan in a way I hadn't before. We'd befriended previous enemies a lot in the past few years, yet they seemed to want me to stay away from her. How many people had tried to kill us and still would if given the chance?

Ginx was a lot of things, but unfortunately for me, I knew more than most that no one could feign indifference like Stan and Duchess.

CHAPTER 7

Fuck Vendettas, Build Relationships

GENESIS

"This is beautiful," I told Pharaoh as I admired the striking skyline while we sat on a moon-kissed Lake Michigan. There was nothing like seeing Chicago at night. "I really missed savoring this view."

"Me too." I didn't have to glance his way to know he was staring at me. Observing me. Still wondering if spending time together like this was a good idea.

"I haven't taken this boat out in a while," he said, as both of us sat at the farthest end of small back table. "I have a yacht, but we didn't need all that space for four people."

My eyes drifted to Noble and his friend, Kennedy, who

he'd invited along tonight. "I'm not sure I'm ready to see him dating a girl seriously."

Pharaoh laughed. "Get used to it. If I don't know shit, I know the look of a man when he's falling for a woman and Noble has been a goner for a while."

Noble and Kennedy where on the opposite end of the boat laughing about something, appearing much older than his fourteen years to me.

"Hmm."

I stopped spying on Noble and looked to Pharaoh. "What does *hmm* mean?"

"I need to have the talk with him. He'll probably lose his virginity to that girl."

I popped him on the shoulder. "You will *not* be talking about our son's non-existent sex life. He's too young."

"I was younger than he was," he countered.

My eyes widened. "And look how many damn kids you had in the process."

Raising his hands in the air, he conceded, "Okay, so point taken. He's too young right now … but hanging around with Kennedy, I give them two more months max."

"I don't like this conversation."

"You act like you don't remember how we were at that age," he teased, his dreads flowing around his face as he laughed.

For a moment, I was distracted by how good his dark gingerbread complexion looked when the moon hit him just right. *And those lips* … I knew for a fact he probably put Vaseline on those mugs before he went to bed because they were too damn soft.

"We were in our twenties, not teenagers," I reminded. "And we probably spent … what, not even an entire forty-eight hours having sex one time. All the other times we just did oral shit."

"Which was still doing something sexual," he pointed out. "They at that age where everything seems heightened, and unlike when we grew up, kids these days got social media telling them the type of person they're supposed to like, how they supposed to act. If a girl be secretly throwin' it at a boy like you used to do me when you were swinging on that pole, lil niggas these days don't stand a chance."

"Boy, please, your recollection of that time in our life is jaded," I scoffed. "I was already too damn nervous to be on the pole, and yeah, I was tryin' to seduce you, but if you remember correctly, I fell the first time I tried to twist myself on that pole to entice yo' hoe ass."

"You ain't gotta save face for me," he taunted. "I always knew you only fell so that I would see if you were okay. Couldn't have one of my finest strippers suing me for unlawful treatment, so I was a gentleman."

My mouth dropped. "A gentleman? Ha! You had me in your office, staring at me in a very non-professional way as you inspected my body for bruises."

"I believe in a very hands-on approach when I'm making sure my product is good?"

"Product?" I waved him off. "Oh, you on a whole other disrespectful level tonight." Yet, even as the words left my mouth, I couldn't deny how good it felt to laugh again. All my problems were still looming in the back of my mind, but I'd missed this … missed *him*.

"You know, after I left your office, I was cornered by Big Titty Tia, throwing it in my face that she had fucked you and warning me not to even try it."

"Wait, Tia?" He laughed. "Man, I ain't never fuck that woman, but I fired her though. She started poppin' up all around Chicago, hiding in bushes and shit."

I placed my hand over my mouth, stifling a laugh. "Quit lyin'."

"I wish I was." He shook his head. "I attended this gala solo one day because two of my BMs were fighting and I wasn't with either one of them. Tia popped up there in a fancy gown and everything, walking around the place telling everybody I was her new man. Security quickly escorted her out, but that only riled up my BMs more."

"Are you talking about Ricki and Kayla?"

He nodded. "Yeah. Kayla and I lost our little girl when she was eight to leukemia."

"I'm so sorry," I told him, clutching my heart. "I didn't know that."

"It's still hard to think about her young life cut short, and Kayla didn't take it well. She went through a couple years of depression before she came to me and asked for some money for plastic surgery. She wanted to reinvent herself, and I just wanted her to be okay since she didn't have much family." He looked to me. "A lot of folks didn't realize that Yaya, the new daycare owner who moved to town years ago, was Kayla, my ex. She didn't look anything like herself, but Ricki knew. She told me it was in Yaya's eyes that she recognized a woman she used to hate for reasons she only understood when Yaya returned. The two of them bonded and started getting close. Now they're married."

"Shut the fuck up!" I exclaimed. "I saw Ricki and our conversation was quick, but friendly and easy. You could tell she was so happy, and when she introduced me to her wife, I had no idea it was Kayla. They both seem great together."

He nodded. "Yeah, they been going hard for years. Ricki was clingy as hell when we were together, but Kayla brings out the best side of her. Some people just connect that way." His eyes held mine when he said that last part, sending tingles down my spine.

"You are nothing but trouble," I muttered, closing my eyes and letting my head fall back. Pharaoh always looked so damn kissable and there was no way I could taste those lips with my son here.

He didn't say anything, and when I opened my eyes seconds later, he was staring at me, his face unreadable. "Noble told me you spend a lot of time in LA," he mentioned.

I swallowed, a little nervous at branching off into a topic we hadn't yet. "I do. When I left Chicago, I escaped to LA and needed a fresh start. I didn't know what to do or who to work for, so I decided to enroll in school even though I was damn near ten years older than most of the incoming freshman."

"You always wanted to go to college," he mentioned.

"I did, but I'm surprised you remembered that."

"No you ain't," he amended. "You know I always remember shit that's important to me."

I cleared my throat. "In college is where I met my best friend, Destiny. You would think I would have nothing in common with her young ass, but we bonded and quickly became soul sisters. She never thought I was older."

"'Cause you look damn good for your age."

I smiled. "Thank you. It took a while for me to admit my age to her, but she didn't judge." I apprehensively studied his eyes. "We even became roommates after college, and I was grateful to land a job at Black Lush headquarters, but before all that, she got a chance to meet Noble when he visited me."

Pharaoh clenched and unclenched his jaw. "Noble already mentioned he grew up in Illinois."

Shit, that boy has a big mouth! "It's okay for you to hate me for what I did. My life hadn't been too bad growing up, but I wanted Noble to be free to make his own choices and not be bogged down with the responsibilities of his family." *And have a safer life without me.* "My cousin raised him in the western suburbs of Chicagoland before they moved closer to the city. He had a normal childhood. However, I was always honest with him about who his father was, but asked him not to approach you."

"He was my son, too," Pharaoh stated. "I wouldn't have forced him into a life that he didn't want, and if you would have asked me if he could be raised by your cousin, I would have agreed."

"I know that now," I said. "And in case you're wondering, I've always been honest with him about my family and yours."

Pharaoh's eyes sparked. "That's why he never seems too surprised to learn much about what I do for a living and how we met."

"I knew he was intelligent beyond his years the moment he started talking," I admitted. "At first, my parents weren't in his life a lot, but they'd lost a son already and I didn't want them to lose a grandchild, too. So even though he never lived with them, they saw him regularly."

Pharaoh glanced over at Noble. "He's a great kid. Reminds me so much of myself."

"I know," I agreed. "We may not have been in each other lives all these years, but I see you every time I look at Noble."

"That's funny," he said, his eyes dropping to my lips when he looked my way again. "I'm starting to notice how much he favors his beautiful mother."

It was a whole ass job to slow my breathing and appear unaffected, but he saw right through my shit if his smirk was any indication. Luckily, we didn't have time to act on our obvious attraction because we were interrupted by Noble.

"Kennedy spilled some red Kool-Aid on her dress and her mom will kill her if it's permanently stained," he explained. "Can you help her in the bathroom?"

I blinked a couple times, switching from aroused woman to save-the-day mom. "Sure, I think I have something in my bag that will help."

As I walked down into the cabin of the boat, I was sure I was wearing a goofy grin on my face.

* * *

PHARAOH

"THANKS FOR TAKING us out on the boat tonight," Noble said, sitting in the seat Genesis had just vacated.

"No problem. It looks like Kennedy is really feelin' you."

He smiled, even though he was trying not to. "She is, but Mom keeps telling me to keep it in my pants every time I see her. I think she's worried I'll turn out like you."

I laughed. "Well, you got my DNA, so she's right to worry. I wouldn't trade my kids for anything, but you're young and you need to be careful. Stay safe and strap up to avoid catching a case and paying child support. That shit ain't what's up, trust me."

Noble blinked. "That was lame as hell."

"You need to stop cursing," I told him. "Your mom is already getting on me about that."

"You curse," he retorted.

"I'm grown."

He outstretched his arms the way I always did when I felt like I ain't do shit wrong. "They curse more on the Disney channel now than what I'm sayin'. And don't tell me we 'bout to have *the talk*? I'm grateful you're tryin' to do this whole fatherly-advice thing, but you and I both know it's too late."

"You ain't having sex with her yet, so don't even act like you know where to put yo' dick."

"We will soon though," he corrected. "A lot of my friends are already doing it."

"Who gives a fuck what everybody else is doin'?" I told him. *Shit.* I really needed to try and curse less around him. I was no angel, and I'd be the first to admit I cussed around my older kids, but if they mama asked me to stop, I tried to listen.

"Okay, so maybe I'm not having sex yet," he disclosed. "But I don't have any questions about it or want some kumbaya moment when I do. Is it cool if I come to you if I have any questions, but you keep it chill?"

"Sure," I lied, knowing he'd been having conversations with his brother, Zayden, who was around the same age, but a little older. No doubt he told Noble about my rituals. I wanted Noble to wait until him and his girlfriend were ready, but when he did start having sex, I'd do the same thing I did with my other sons. I'd bring out the cigars, a shot of Patrón, and play Like Father, Like Son one and two by The Game and Busta Rhymes while we sat on my back patio vibing to that shit. Especially with Noble since I had to make up for lost time. Not only was it a good bonding experience, but I could lay down the law of being careful and safe, while also respecting boundaries in a way they related to a little more.

When it came to my daughters, fuck a celebration, I was collecting names of whatever lil nigga thought he was man enough to sleep with one of my babies. Talk reckless about her and you were liable to get fucked up.

I wouldn't win father of the year, but my kids knew they could come to me for anything and I had their back.

"My mom was telling me I'm an uncle, too," Noble mentioned. "So I have eleven siblings and how many nieces and nephews?"

"Three nieces and two nephews," I told him. "Your oldest sister, Seyra, had triplets, and the other kids stepped in to help her and her husband raise them since they are a lot to handle. I think it worked as the best form of birth control." I lifted an eyebrow at Noble. "I'm planning an end of summer barbecue next month. I already told your mom, and she said you can go, but maybe you should meet the triplets before you decide to take things further with Kennedy."

He laughed. "How about we make a deal?"

"Nah, I don't make deals with kids, especially my own."

"I'll watch the triplets after school for a whole week," he said, ignoring me, "if you finally tell my mom she can help with whatever she's been bugging you about."

"Did your mom tell you the situation?"

He shook his head. "No. I just heard her talking to her friend, Des, and she mentioned you hadn't agreed to let her help despite how close y'all were getting."

"You know too damn much for your age," I told him. "I knew that from the day of the reception when you picked up on the fact that I was trying to place your mom's name."

He looked surprised. "I should be asking why you decided to test me when it was obvious when my mom approached you after I went to dance with Kennedy that you'd never forgotten who she was and was faking it."

"Anyone can pretend to pick up on certain behaviors and social cues, but only a few have a rare gift to understand the motives of others within a few minutes of meeting."

"Since I'm so perceptive for my age, does that mean we have a deal?" he asked.

"Your mom and I have a complicated relationship."

"I know," he answered, his voice sincere. "My mom always thinks she made a mistake by not being around as much as she would have liked, but she's always been the best. Nurturing, despite how tough she is. Caring, although she doesn't always want others to see it. But I think she needs you now. I don't know what's going on with my mom, but whatever it is, if you love her, you'll help her, not push her away. If you don't have the time, spend less time with me and focus on her."

"I would never do that," I told him, clasping him on the shoulder, taken aback by his selflessness when it came to his mom. "And since meeting your mom, there's never been a point in my life where I didn't have time to spend with her." *Hell, she had all my damn focus when she wasn't even trying.*

"You'll help her then?" His eyes were hopeful, yet confident, like he already knew I would agree to do whatever I needed to do for Genesis. "Regardless of what's going on?"

"I will," I told him, truly meaning it.

Smiling, he nodded his head. "Good. And for the record, I'm not one of those kids who secretly hope that their parents get married or anything, but in case you wanted to know my thoughts, I'm cool with that if you both want to try again. Just make sure you not knocking her up anytime soon, 'cause I'm still trying to get all the siblings, nieces, and nephews straight. Had to make a list and er'thang."

I couldn't stop the laugh that consumed me. "Appreciate the blessing." Conversation was a lot more lighthearted after that, but I didn't miss the sly look on Genesis' face as she stood next to me while I sailed back to the Chicago Yacht Club.

"Might as well tell me what you're thinking instead of staring at me."

She ran her fingers down the exposed part of my arm. "Thanks for letting me work with you to end Boris."

"I ain't even say shit about that all night."

"You're letting me help," she said. "It's written all over your face, and I just want you to know I appreciate it."

When I glanced her way, sincerity and appreciation were reflected in her eyes. The moment was sweet, but my thoughts were far from that. All I wanted to do was fuck her over this railing and see what was underneath that tight-fitted, green, cotton dress that shouldn't have looked so fucking sexy when we weren't alone for me to do shit about it.

I made a mental note right then and there to make sure the next time we took this boat for a spin, we'd leave the kids at home.

CHAPTER 8

Fuck Small Fish, Go for Broke

PHARAOH

"Hellooooooo, Mexico!" Hollis exclaimed for the tenth time since we landed.

"Nigga, get in the damn car so we can go." I popped him in his arm and slid into the passenger seat while Jock got behind the wheel. "We're supposed to keep a low profile while we're here," I reminded him. "Can you at least try and act like you've been to Mexico before?"

"Why do you think I'm so goddamn excited?" he exclaimed. "Do you know how long it's been since I last seen Yasmin? Five years! I told her to wait for me, and she said she'd be the first one to greet me next time we were in town. I sent her a Facebook message when we landed to meet me at the restaurant."

"Fool, that woman ain't wait around for you," Jock goaded, hopping on the highway to meet with my contact at an outdoor restaurant on the beach strip in Tulum, Mexico. "Wasn't she the one who neither one of y'all could understand each other?"

"We didn't need words with a connection as strong as ours," Hollis claimed, linking his hands behind his head as he slightly leaned back. "Last time I was here, we spent days laying on the beach making love as discreetly as possible. It was one of the best times of my life."

Jock and I shared a look before I reminded Hollis that, "You say that shit every time you're with a woman. They can't all be the best time of your life."

He frowned. "Listen, I make forever, lasting memories with my ladies. You lay with women and pop babies, I lay with women and grow my list of maybes. Can't just any female become Mrs. Hennessey. So let me be great and focus on your own shit."

"We're here to work," I reminded him. "Just make sure you don't spend the next three days all up under Yasmin's skirt."

"Whateva!"

WITH TRAFFIC, construction, several unavoidable potholes, and Hollis' constant need to piss every thirty minutes from drinking too much rum and Coke on the plane, it took us a long three hours to get to Tulum beach strip.

"Never again," Jock muttered to me when we parked in a dirt lot down the street from the restaurant we were supposed to arrive at an hour prior.

"I know," I said with a laugh. "Now you see why we

make Hennessey drive by himself to anyplace over thirty minutes."

"Fuck that," Jock huffed. "His ass got a five-minute limit before I kick him out of the car next time if he acts like a damn child unable to hold his piss."

Dodging a few cars and mopeds on the narrow street, we walked to the restaurant, forcing Hollis to keep walking since his ass wanted to take photos in front of the Ven a La Luz wooden sculpture created by South African artist Daniel Popper.

"Oh, man, I can just see Yasmin already," Hollis mentioned, rubbing his hands together as we waited for traffic to slow so we could cross the street. "I wonder if she still has those same thick thighs and hypnotizing light brown eyes. She was growing her hair out five years ago, so I bet it's long as hell now. So long, I can probably wrap my—" Hollis stopped mid-stride and jumped back into one of the entryways to a small villa.

"What the hell are you doing?" I asked, shaking my head at how we could only see half his face while the rest stayed hidden.

"Yo, does that look like Yasmin to y'all?"

I looked to where he was pointing at a woman who'd just gotten out of a car. "Yeah, that looks like the woman I remember."

"And do those three creatures pulling on her arm look like they belong to her or the person who dropped her off?"

"Damn," Jock snorted. "Those must be her kids."

"Noooooooooooo!" Hollis yelled, his hiding spot forgotten as he dropped to his knees, yelling into the sky like he'd just lost his best friend.

"Nigga, get the fuck up," Jock prompted, grabbing

ahold of his arm while I grasped the other one. "You got us out here lookin' crazy as hell."

"Y'all my brothers," Hollis screeched. "Y'all know how devastating it is to witness that."

Jock shook his head and threw his hands up. "How many times I got to tell you? I'm Pharaoh's brother, not yours. We ain't related, bruh."

"Same difference," Hollis retorted, continuing to look up at the sky like someone was playing a cruel joke on him.

"No it aint!" Jock shouted. "It's not the same."

Hollis ignored him and continued talking. "And as my brother, you need to be a little more fuckin' considerate right now."

I glanced Yasmin's way as she turned around, looking down the street to see what all the commotion was. She almost saw us, but one of the kids tugged on her arm and she turned to talk to the hostess.

"You in the clear," I told Hollis, helping him brush off some dirt. "So quit being so goddamn dramatic."

"Dramatic!" Hollis exclaimed. "I have a right to be when the love of my life never disclosed anything about having kids in our Facebook messages."

"Hennessey, quit with that shit," I told him. "She wasn't the love of your life."

He waved me off. "Love of my life. Love at the time. Love at the moment. You act like you don't give a fuck that my heart is bleeding."

I pinched the bridge of my nose. "You're giving me a muthafuckin' headache.

"You still pissin' me off," Jock said. "But, when was the last time you saw her again?"

"Five years ago," Hollis whined, still distraught. "Why do you ask?"

I followed Jock's gaze. "Hate to tell you this, bruh, but

that older kid is looking a little tanner than the others, don't you think?"

"Huh?" Hollis stopped being a little bitch and peeped what we were referring to. "Shit. Lil dude does look like he can be half Black, right?" Hollis started light jogging across the street. "Hey, yo, Yasmin, baby! It's me! Henny! I've come to see you and finally meet my son."

Yasmin's face slightly dropped, then widened into a smile as she hugged Hollis, planting kisses all over his face, while her kids hugged Hollis around his legs.

"He got problems," Jock observed. "How the fuck he go from devastated she got kids, to claiming one of them is his?"

I shook my head, laughing. "Nah, I'm more concerned with how those kids already acting like he they damn daddy."

"Fellas!" Hollis yelled. "Come meet my family!"

"What?" Jock huffed, leaning to me. "Is this dumb ass for real?"

My smile dropped. "Shit. Let's get over there before he really run off and get married. Duchess would kill my ass if her baby boy falls into a situation."

Jock cursed the whole walk over.

* * *

"OF COURSE he has to be my son," Hollis stated after spending the past two hours wining and dining Yasmin and her three kids until she said she had to go and promised to meet up with him later.

"Bruh, why the hell do you assume that?" I asked.

He gave me a look like it was obvious. "How many Black dudes you think she fuckin' in Mexico?"

Constantine scratched the back of his head while the

two men standing by Jock were trying not to laugh. I was relieved to learn Constantine had also been running late and needed to switch the meeting location to Mistico, a hookah bar and restaurant across the city, because had he not, we never could have pried Hollis away from Yasmin.

Constantine "Niko" Hood was not only a friend, but one of the business partners that I trusted with my life. He was from Detroit before he moved to Mexico to join his brother's cartel. Half Black, half Mexican, all hood. We'd been through a lot of shit together and lived to agree that some stories were so fucked up, they were better left untold.

"Why y'all laughing like that?" Hollis asked, glancing around the room.

"Let's just say, Yasmin has always attracted a lot of men," Constantine implied.

Hollis' eyes widened. "Get the fuck outta here! You tellin' me my innocent señorita who called me her trueno de chocolate had several others?"

"Her what?" Jock interrupted.

"Her chocolate thunder," one of the guys answered. "What Yasmin calls all the tourists she manages to get her hands on when they come to Tulum."

Hollis squinted at the guy. "Why are you talkin' like you've been with Yasmin?"

He didn't say anything. Just laughed. Then the other guy laughed.

"Please tell me you both ain't been wit' my girl."

The first guy shrugged. "Okay, we won't say it."

Hollis dropped his head onto the table, his fedora surprisingly staying in place. "Jesus, let it not be my Latin cutie that gave up the booty." He looked to me with that look I knew all too well. My reflexes were good, but I swear, Henny's ass be quick. "Hold me bruh … Tight."

My arms flew around him to keep myself from falling since he slammed into me so hard. I started to push his goofy ass off me, but Hollis was a hugger, so instead, I found myself saying, "You were too good for her anyway, man."

"I was, wasn't I?" he mumbled.

Shit, this fucker is worse than my kids. After a minute, shit felt weird, so I carefully dislodged myself from his tight ass hug and motioned for Jock to take him out of the room so I could have a civilized business conversation. Originally, Hollis was supposed to be a part of the discussion, but his ass was going through too many misplaced emotions right now.

"Come on, man," Jock said, gently patting his shoulder. "Let's get you a drink."

"With a little umbrella in it?" Hollis asked, looking like a sad puppy.

"I'll tell them to give you two umbrellas," Jock answered. Jock could complain all he wanted, but he had a soft spot for Hollis just like we all did.

The other guys followed Jock out at Constantine's order.

"I've lived all over the world," he said. "And I ain't never come across anyone like Hennessey before. When he was a kid, I thought he'd grow outta that overly dramatic shit."

"Nah, he ain't never changing."

Constantine laughed. "You think I should have told him that Yasmin already knows who the dad is for her oldest?"

I shook my head. "It won't make a difference. He has to work through his feelings, and even though he won't admit it, he's already over Yasmin."

"On that note," he said, motioning for us to take a seat at a table in the corner of the private room.

"We good to talk here?"

Constantine placed his hand over his chest like he was offended. "Come on, man. You know me betta than that."

"I gotta triple check how secure shit is these days," I told him.

"I feel you." His phone rang, interrupting the conversation. "Give me a minute."

"No problem."

I expected him to step out to take the call, but he stood off to the corner of the room and answered. I occupied myself by taking my iPad out of my bag and opened the beta Velvet app, trying not to ear hustle, but words like, "hey princess" and "not until I meet their parents" caught my attention.

"So, uh, princess, huh?" I asked, after he disconnected the call.

"Yeah, man. I don't get how you keep track of all your kids when it's hard for me to be a dad to one of them without psychoanalyzing every friend she makes and doing a thorough background check on their parents."

"Hold up, I know you have a son, but since when do you have a daughter?"

He smiled. "You remember Stella from back in the day?"

I laughed. "The one you broke up with every damn week until she finally got smart and left yo' ass for that doctor?"

He frowned. "Ion know about all that, but yeah, that Stella."

"She ain't tell you?" I asked, thinking about Genesis and Noble who were never far from my mind lately.

"Well, her husband passed away and she popped up

when I was in Detroit for a visit several years back, claiming she wanted me to meet her daughter. I was pissed as hell for a while, but Aria is one of the best things to come out of that fucked up relationship we had. She loved Stella's husband, but her and I have gotten close, too."

"Damn." I shook my head. "I remember when you used to say you never wanted to have a daughter because if she ended up with a muthafucka like us, you were liable to kill him on sight."

His face dropped. "And I meant that shit."

"Having daughters is different than sons," I told him. "A daughter changes your perspective on shit you used to never think twice about."

"She's already changed my whole world," he admitted. "I can't imagine something happening to her like what happened to …" His voice trailed off, but he didn't need to finish his sentence. Some tragedies were never far from your heart. "I want to make this world safer for my daughters."

"I feel that to my core," I told him, clasping a hand on his shoulder. "And we will."

Clearing my throat, I slid him the iPad, the mood in the room shifting even more as I did so.

"Is this it?" Constantine asked, his face growing serious and his brows furrowed.

"Yeah. Hennessey and I have gone through every part of it to make sure it's exactly what we need it to be, but we wanted to make sure you and Cristobal are good to go moving forward here in Mexico."

His face grew serious as he observed the app, emotion he didn't try to hide from me seeping through. Cristobal De León was Constantine's half-brother through his mother and leader of a cartel group that operated out of Tulum. In our world, we were all bad, but some were worse than others. Cristo's father, Diego, had wanted to make a difference in the world. He'd been one of the good cartel leaders, respect earned in ways I still admired to this day.

Constantine and I used to travel to Mexico all the time back in the day, welcomed by Diego. To Diego, it didn't matter that Constantine had a different father. The De Leons quickly became allies of the Crownes through our connection with Constantine and his other Hood family. In a way, we felt on top of the world back then when we visited the country. Until Cristo's father was killed and Cristo and Constantine's sister, Carmen, was captured.

That was the day Cristo became El Jefe, leader of his father's cartel.

"I know we've discussed this at length," I told him. "But through the Velvet app, I'm confident we will expose several human trafficking organizations who have been responsible for an increase in cases, especially here in Mexico. The country is hot right now, and law enforcement is either limited, or on payroll. The soft launch was extremely informative, but we'll have to act fast after the launch. Anyone scrolling through the fake profiles we have set up are informed that transactions won't be fulfilled until three months from now. The strip clubs should support the ruse for those digging deeper into how Velvet operates, and all seven strip clubs will be open before the deadline."

"Delilah is doing well," he said, referring to the strip club outside of Tulum we co-owned. "We've even had a few men who were on the list you sent me visit the location to lay eyes on the women."

"That's good," I told him. "You'll have to talk to Cristo about enhancing security measures on all the women as I have for the other locations as well."

"I can't believe so many women are willing to help for the cause."

I nodded. "I was, too. It's a sticky situation running strip clubs and gentlemen lounges with a background app that targets the very men and women we want to keep our employees from. However, the app only has profiles for the women who were placed undercover at the strip clubs. Survivors or family of victims."

Constantine clasped his hands together. "I know we've been talking about this for years, but it almost seems unreal to finally have the app here." He looked at the iPad, hope in his eyes. "Cristo and I are realistic. Carmen may not be alive. But I don't want anyone to go through what we went through."

"The best way to catch the human traffickers who captured Carmen is through this app," I stated. "I'm confident of that."

"How will the transactions work?"

We both turned at the knock on the door, Constantine standing to question who it was, but shaking his head the minute we heard, "Can you assholes open the door? Jock and the others are starting to annoy me."

Annoy him? Pretty sure it was the other way around.

"Thanks for finally showing the fuck up," I teased as he walked into the room.

"Fuck you, I had to work through some shit." He pulled up a chair and took a seat at the table. "What did I miss?"

"Constantine was just asking how the transactions would work."

"I got you." After pulling his laptop out his book bag, he started typing in some shit as he explained, "This is the backend of the app. I've placed a tracking code in every account holder's profile so that as soon as they put in a request, I'll be able to follow their every move, even when they leave the site."

"What if they use an untraceable device?" Constantine asked.

"That's the beauty this code," I stated. "Hennessey was able to create coding to reverse any untraceable code another hacker may enter in the system. He's basically pretending to play the system we created to give anyone who may be apprehensive security in thinking they succeeded in blocking how we track their movement."

"Not exactly the way I would have explained it," Hollis claimed, "but that's the proudest you've ever made me, almost talking a coder's language and shit."

I shrugged. "On occasion, I listen to shit you say when it's important to me."

Hollis went on to explain everything in more detail, including the fake identities he had to create for the women undercover. After almost three hours, we were confident that we had everything in place for a successful launch.

"Okay, fellas. As much as I'd love to shoot the shit with y'all after this heavy discussion, I got a date with Yas." He packed up his stuff and started dancing to the door.

"Wait, did you just say you got a date with Yasmin?" Constantine asked.

"Yeah," he confirmed, wiggling his eyebrows. "And this time, she's leaving her kids at home." He looked to me. "I'm gonna head to our place and freshen up."

"Okay."

After Hollis left, Constantine was still looking from me to the door, with his mouth slightly open. "I just don't understand him."

"Don't try to," I cautioned. "Jock and I will trail his ass, but at least he said they were *her* kids this time and not his."

I looked to the door. "You know what, since we're done for the day, maybe I should go after him now."

Constantine nodded. "Yeah, fool! No offense, but he ain't wrapped too tight when it comes to that woman."

"Right."

I walked out of that place with a goal to make sure Hollis didn't do anything stupid, but my mind was on the woman who made me do reckless shit, too.

In the end, it always comes down to a woman.

CHAPTER 9

Fuck Overthinking, Go With the Flow

GENESIS

"You see, this is exactly what I needed," I told Selena, a friend that I'd met through Destiny as we laid on a beach in Tulum, Mexico. I had barely dropped my bags off in the chic villa before Selena and I ran outside so I could dip my toes in the water.

"You work too hard," she told me, adjusting herself on the day bed so that the sun could kiss as much of her body as possible. "Besides, I appreciate the distraction before things get too crazy out here."

I nodded, not bringing up the real reason I'd come to Mexico. Destiny was supposed to be with us, but she wasn't arriving until tomorrow.

"How do you like living in Mexico?" I asked. Selena was born and raised in California, but had moved to Mexico a year ago.

"Like every place, it has its pluses and minuses, but I've been enjoying myself. Just wish I was here under different circumstances.

"I know." Movement out of the corner of my eye caught my attention. "Not to change the subject, but didn't you say this beach was private?"

"It is," she confirmed, sitting upright on the bed and raising her hand over her face to block the sun. "But that's not a trespasser. That's the owner of this villa."

She stood, and I followed suit, my eyes glued to two men walking our way … both tall, broad shouldered, and with unmistakable features that made them easy to identify, even if I was in another country. *And now it's time to put what I learned in that acting class to good use.*

"What the fuck kinda sick joke is this?" I said aloud as I gave Constantine a tight hug before going to Pharaoh next, my stomach in knots at seeing him.

Constantine placed his hand on his chin, teasing when he said, "Nah, this can't be that same skinny girl who used to visit her aunt in Detroit claiming to be the best at shooting dice."

I was already shaking my head since he always brought up the same shit every time I saw him. "I *was* better at shooting dice than you and probably still *am*. You and your cousins just hated to be beat by a girl."

Even though I used to slay in a good dress back then, I'd always been a tomboy at heart, but it was awkward being myself. Constantine had treated me just as I'd longed to be treated. Like my own person without any labels.

"Constantine told me he thought you were friends with

Selena," Pharaoh stated. "Didn't even know you and Niko kept in touch."

I crossed my arms over my chest, sensing a hint of jealousy that shouldn't have made me feel good, but it did. "That's because you assume you know everything about everyone, when truth is, people are multi-layered."

He chuckled, leaning down to whisper, "Ginx, I could spend the rest of my life exploring every delicious inch of you and still find a hidden layer you thought no one would discover."

Word? My eyes dropped to his lips because how could they not? On their own accord, they continued going down his body, admiring his khaki-colored shorts, white tee, and bare feet before making my way back up to his dreads that were pulled back.

He looks damn good. It was a little hard to pretend not to be affected by him standing in front of me right now.

Not sure how long I stood there with a goofy smile on my face before Selena asked, "How do you know Niko?"

"From back in the day," I explained, shaking off my arousal. "I used to visit his neighborhood a lot when I was younger. We met through my brother." I almost whispered the last word, looking to Pharaoh as I did so, the elephant that was always in the room with us, lingering in the warm, humid breeze. His eyes didn't show a hint of sorrow, but even if he had been sorry, he'd been trained all his life not to show regret when it came to choices he deemed necessary for the bigger picture.

Clearing my throat, I looked from Constantine to Selena. "How exactly do y'all know each other?"

"Constantine and I share the same sister," Selena explained, my heart clutching at the sadness in her voice. "Although Carmen and I share the same father, we have different mothers."

"Whereas Carmen and I have the same mother," Constantine added. "Basically, Selena's family."

"I'm so sorry about Carmen," I told Constantine. "When Selena first told me, I couldn't believe it. I never met her, but Selena always talks about her."

I'd never known any of Constantine's relatives on his mom's side, only his dad's. Still, I couldn't help but feel like if I hadn't been so focused on my own shit lately, I would have noticed this much earlier.

Even more mind-boggling was the fact that Selena and I weren't from as different of a world as I thought if she was connected to Niko's family. Granted, I didn't mind growing closer in our friendship with this added connection, but it was all just … complicated when I wasn't trying to lay all my cards out on the table.

Constantine nodded. "I appreciate it. If she's alive, we plan on getting her back, no matter what it takes."

I noticed the way Selena winced when he said *if* she's alive, but I knew enough about Constantine to know he operated in facts, and when it came to human trafficking for a victim who'd been gone for years, odds weren't usually good.

"I came to see how you were," Constantine told Selena. "Everything is going according to plan."

"Good," she stated. "I'm not nervous, but I'm ready to nail these bastards."

Constantine looked hesitantly to me.

"Genesis knows," Selena told him, peeping the stare.

"For the record," I added, "I asked Carmen if she needed more women to go undercover for whatever operation you two have going on."

The three of them glanced between one another in a way that made me feel like the last to know, prompting me to ask, "What am I missing?"

"It's a lot to explain," Pharaoh stated. "Constantine told me you're staying here at the villa, so how about we head inside and I'll explain over dinner? The chef can whip up anything we want."

"Sure," I said. "If it's okay with Constantine that we use his chef. It was nice of him to let us have the whole place this weekend."

Pharaoh glanced back at Constantine, both laughing before Pharaoh enlightened that, "I own the villa, Genesis. Selena and I haven't known each other long, but she told me she needed a couple rooms for a girls' weekend, and I said no problem since I rent out most of them anyway. Constantine owns plenty of properties they could use, this just happens to be mine."

"With one of the best views of this beach," Selena pointed out, wiggling her eyebrows.

"Are you staying here, too?" I asked, which was stupid because he owned it, so of course he was.

He confirmed anyway, and I couldn't deny the thrill I felt knowing he was staying in the same villa as I was.

"Well, I guess we can all go inside then," I announced, clasping my hands together, not liking so much attention on me.

"Not me," Constantine declared. "I got some shit to handle."

"Me too," Selena added quickly. "And before you ask, I was gonna tell you I had to go handle something for a little bit, but that I'd be back."

I had a feeling she was lying, yet, when Pharaoh stepped aside and motioned for me to walk ahead of him back into the villa, I found myself smiling.

"You didn't seem shocked to see me," I told him after the chef informed us he could have dinner ready in an hour. We were seated at the sleek, wooden table in multipurpose room, decorated in beachy jungle décor.

"Niko told me right before we arrived that you were here after Selena mentioned it."

"Gotcha. Still crazy that Selena and Niko share a sister though."

Pharaoh nodded. "It is. In our line of work, we hear a lot of shit, but Niko was devastated when Carmen was taken."

"Selena didn't tell me too many details, just enough. I sensed she was holding back, but eventually she opened up about Carmen being kidnapped by a friend of the family."

"A rival cartel group," Pharaoh corrected. "But later, it was discovered who they work for is much more complicated. The rival cartel may track and smuggle people, but weren't the ones calling the shots. The Crownes have been trying to get rid of a particular human trafficking group for years and our mission aligned with our allies, so we've been actively working to expose those involved. I'm spearheading several avenues we're taking to do this."

"Wait … Selena mentioned going undercover as a bartender at Delilah here in Tulum for a boss who plans on exposing those who smuggle women against their will. I assume Constantine is that boss?"

"Constantine and I co-own Delilah," he explained. "And you know I opened Scarlet in Chicago. I have several others opening too, which will all be functioning gentlemen lounges, and serve as a ruse as well."

For a brief second, I contemplated on being honest with Pharaoh and telling him how closely our goals aligned even if my loyalty to the cause would be questioned based off the information I shared.

He was being so honest with me, just like he had back

when we met. *And just like years ago, you can't be fully honest with him.*

"I told Selena that I wouldn't mind talking to the owner of Delilah to see if I could assist, and she brushed me off, claiming she didn't want to jeopardize my safety when I have a child."

"She was right," he said, his eyes hinting that he'd noticed my inner struggle. With what, he wasn't sure. "We're taking every precaution possible to ensure the safety of our employees, undercover or not. There's even an app that will give us an added layer on intel. However, this is all a risk that may not pay off how we want."

"It will," I encouraged, reaching over the table and gentle squeezing his hands, impressed to learn yet another layer of Pharaoh's character that I wasn't aware of, but not surprised in the least. "Yeah, it's dangerous, but sometimes, you have to risk big to win big."

"Exactly." His mouth was saying one thing, but his eyes were saying, "Some things aren't worth the risk though." He didn't have to voice the words for me to know the direction of his thoughts.

"What's the app about?" I asked.

He leaned back in his chair and observed me in a way that let me know he was contemplating if telling me was the right decision based on his suspicion that I was withholding information while he was being an open book.

Apparently deciding it was okay, he divulged the information about the app and the part it played in the overall goal.

"That's impressive," I told him. "Then again, I'm not shocked because there was always more to you than what meets the eye."

"What aren't you telling me?" he asked, apparently

done watching me hesitate when I realized I almost revealed too much.

"Nothing that concerns you," I lied.

"Bullshit." He stood quicker than I could react, my breath catching when he stopped behind me. "How long have you been planning to be in Mexico? Since before you walked back into my life or only after we reconnected?"

"Before," I admitted. "I really had no idea Selena and Constantine were related until today."

"You knew I was in Mexico though?"

I nodded, not because of nerves, but because I'd told so many lies, my truths were now questionable. "I did."

He leaned down to my ear, his voice sending a shiver down my spine when he voiced, "And yet, you still followed me into this villa knowing Constantine and Selena wouldn't blink an eye to save you if I killed you right now?"

"That's true." Selena was my friend, but I knew how close Constantine and Pharaoh were. No doubt Selena would choose her family, blood or not, over a friend with more secrets than bodies buried at a cemetery.

For years, I'd spent time perfecting my facial expressions and ability to let lies flow easily off my tongue. *Not with Pharaoh though.* In more ways than one, he'd been my kryptonite. A chip in armor that was otherwise unscathed.

"I can't tell you what you want to hear," I admitted. "Not yet anyway."

"Why not?" he asked. "You don't think waiting fifteen years for the goddamn truth about you ain't long enough?"

"It is."

"But?"

I took a deep breath. "But I can't tell—"

"At least tell me this," he demanded, cutting me off and leaning over enough where I could see the profile of his face. "Despite our history and the son we share, does a part of you still want to kill me?"

Yes. The truth was at the tip of my tongue, but refused to be voiced. By not responding immediately, I'd given him an answer. Which begged the question, "Do you ever wish you'd finished the job and killed me after you killed my brother?"

He didn't answer either, but he didn't have to. The reality of our situation had always been too messy to ignore, more so for me than him since I'd always known there would be no happy ending for us from the time his eyes landed on me in the strip club.

"I do, but not for reasons you think," he confessed, shocking the hell out of me. "I told you I never wanted to kill your brother, but he left me no choice." Pharaoh pushed the hair off my neck, a lone finger trailing down the slope. "Yet, the reason I wish I'd killed you sometimes is because a man like me can't afford a weakness like you in my life, my feelings for you a flaw in every way possible."

My eyes flew to his, unable to comprehend why he'd been so brutally honest. "You weren't supposed to tell me that."

"I can say whatever the fuck I wanna say," he spat, kissing the spot right behind my earlobe. "You tracked me here to Mexico, didn't you?"

I nodded as his tongue grazed my neck next. "Yes. I needed to make sure you weren't leaving me out of the plan to eliminate Boris."

"Only half true." Twisting my chair, he turned it away from the table so that I was facing him. His eyes studied mine. "You also came because you're trying to find a friend."

My lips slightly parted, my eyes unable to hide their

surprise. "She's been missing for the same amount of time as Carmen has. She was vacationing in Mexico before she went missing."

"Not quite," he challenged. "She went missing around the same time, but not in Mexico. Somewhere else. But you knew I'd be in Mexico, and Selena told you how she planned on helping Carmen, so you figured it was worth a shot." He dragged his thumb over my bottom lip. "I'm guessing you asked your friend, Destiny, to arrive a day later so you could question Selena and make sure everything was legit."

For a few seconds, I didn't say anything. Couldn't say anything. He was on the ball about so much.

"How did you …" My voice trailed off from disbelief, unable to gather my thoughts and save face.

"We're all on the same team when it comes to this, Ginx." His hand gently grazed my cheek, and my heart was beating out of my chest when he said, "You just need to decide if you'll start being honest with me, or if whatever kind of relationship we have for the sake of Noble will be a tug-a-war for information."

"My friend and I haven't had any luck finding her sister," I admitted. "At this point, anytime we hear someone working to eliminate human trafficking, we actively seek out more intel."

"How did you meet your friend?" I asked.

I briefly closed my eyes, knowing that question would come soon after what I disclosed. "I can't answer that."

"Won't answer it."

"Same difference." When he lowered his head to mine, I was a ball of confusion wrapped in a shiny layer of arousal for reasons that didn't make sense. The last thing I needed to do right now was kiss Pharaoh with the way things were, and yet, as he pulled me from that chair and lifted me onto the table, I didn't give a damn if it was wrong or not.

"You fuckin' up, Ginx," he muttered, lifting my dress and snapping my panties with a strength that still made me lose my fucking mind every time he did that. I may be without quite a few panties, but the thrill I got when he popped the fabric in two took my desire up several notches.

"I only fuck up when it pertains to you," I said honestly. Pharaoh may run the streets of Chicago, but I'd spent most of my life working for people who wanted to remain unknown, while hiding in plain sight.

I wanted to tell him everything. Who I worked for. Who I was. Why his and my path always seemed to cross as fate's sick way of making me question everything I thought I knew in this world.

I kept my mouth shut, though. The complications that could arise from disclosing information too soon weighed heavy on my mind as he untied the top of my dress and sucked a nipple into his mouth after the material drifted to my waist.

He didn't go to remove my bra, but we both knew there was a pistol strapped to the back band, just like I knew he wouldn't fully drop his pants to the floor to avoid his Glock being close.

Looking back, it had always been like this between us. Chemistry unmatched, yet trust questionable. Maybe if it had been different from the start, we both could allow ourselves to be more vulnerable, starting with getting completely naked, unbothered by who would be the first to disrobe when uncertainty was heightened.

My hands roamed under his white tee, his tattoos teasing me, waiting for my tongue to lick them clean from the salty sweat of being in the Mexico sun all day. My mouth could only reach the tattoo that snuck up the side of his neck, my lips parched for his taste and his taste only.

I moaned when his fingers found my clit, my juices drenching his hand as he suckled that spot on my neck that drove me crazy. Shamelessly grinding against his hand, I didn't even give a shit that we were on the main floor of the villa with a chef a couple doors down.

The delicious scent of the aromas of our dinner wafted through my nostrils, causing my stomach to growl.

"Damn, guess we should have waited until after I feed you," he teased.

"Absolutely not," I shot back, groaning when he removed his hand, but quickly changing my tone when he pulled out that thick and dripping dick that I often thought about in my dreams.

"Shit," he huffed. "I gotta see if I have a condom in my suite."

I waved him off. "Fuck that. I'm on the pill."

No sooner had the words left my mouth than he was sliding into me, my pussy slowly widening to accommodate his size.

"Oh fuck," I huffed, adjusting myself on the table and hoping I didn't break the thing in the process.

"You ain't tryin' to take this dick for real," he voiced huskily in my ear.

"Don't play wit' me."

"Who the fuck playin'?" he asked. "Don't tell a nigga he don't need a condom, then be afraid to feel that shit all in your gut."

"Ain't nobody scared."

"Show me then, shit." He began kneading his thumbs on the inside of my thighs in slow, marvelous circles. Once my thighs were more relaxed, he continued easing inside of me as I opened for him.

Taking a deep breath, I relaxed my legs and pussy muscles even more as those last inches filled me. *Ohmydamn.* Of course I'd been with other men in the fifteen years we'd been apart, but there was something so fucking delicious about the way Pharaoh moved inside of me.

We were just getting started, but I already knew if I wasn't careful, I'd forget all the reasons why we could never work.

* * *

PHARAOH

HER PUSSY FELT JUST as phenomenal as I remembered. Warm. Wet. Perfectly crafted to fit my dick once I was buried deep inside. I kissed the Ankh symbol right behind her left ear, twirling my tongue around the tattoo like I always did.

It made no damn sense to let a woman like Genesis not just get close to me once, but twice. Especially when she had so many damn secrets. Even though Constantine had given me the heads-up that she was in Tulum, I hadn't expected to see her rocking that peach dress with braids in her hair that she hadn't had last time we saw each other.

I'd wanted to fuck her on sight, but her being there wasn't a coincidence. When it came to Genesis, she may seem like the kind of woman who grew up in the streets like I did, but there had always been more to her than that. Shit about her that didn't truly add up if I really thought back to that time we'd met, set up or not.

Although Hollis was great at digging up information

about folks, to find out more about Ginx, I had reached out to Malik Madden, the brother of Carter Madden, a man who was friends with Saint, Hollis, Creed, and Jedidiah from their military days.

We'd run into each other a few times in Chicago, and Malik was one of those loyal cats who I didn't have to worry about spreading my business if I hired him for shit. He was a PI with a law enforcement background, and even though I usually didn't trust a blue suit, I'd hired him before and he'd proven himself trustworthy.

It took him a week or so to find information on Genesis that wasn't fabricated. That in itself was a dead giveaway that after all this time, she was still lying to me. He hadn't found much, but he'd found enough for me to know when she purchased a flight to Mexico and that she'd hired someone to track my movement.

Problem was, pussy didn't lie and she wanted me just as much as I wanted her. We got into a steady rhythm, her hips coming off the table to meet me stroke for stroke. Everything about her felt addictive. Like any pussy I previously had was just mediocre as my dick waited for the chance to feel her again. Familiarize myself with her moans and groans she made during sex.

When she cried out loud, head thrashed backwards and legs shaking from a powerful orgasm, I followed soon after, shooting my nut so far up her pussy, I was thankful she was on birth control.

We were both sticky as I leaned my forehead against hers, our breathing still labored. Usually, I always knew what to say, but words escaped me as I stared into the deep brown depths of her eyes, noting that even after all this time, my body still reacted to her more than anyone I'd met in my entire life.

I also saw a hint of sadness and vulnerability. From what, I wasn't sure. She opened her mouth to speak, but gasped when she spotted something behind me.

I quickly turned, both of us pulling out our pistols and pointing it to the direction of the balcony. Once I saw what it was, I lowered my gun and secured my pants as Genesis followed suit and adjusted her dress while the cracked door slid fully open.

"Hollis, what the fuck are you doing in here?"

He outstretched his hands. "I ain't even do shit. I was minding my own business, eating my muthafuckin sandwich, when you two burst in and started fucking each other."

"You could have said some shit."

He frowned. "Y'all fuckin' in a public area in the villa, but I can't watch?"

I glanced around, cursing under my breath at the fact that I didn't even remember we were still in the main part of villa, too busy getting whipped by pussy I'd never truly forgotten.

"You should have fuckin' told us," I huffed, securing my shorts. "You lucky we ain't shoot yo' ass, bruh."

Hollis took another bite of his sandwich, observing Genesis, his normal annoying banter obsolete in whatever silent exchange him and Genesis were doing.

"Nice to meet you," Genesis finally said, looking slightly nervous for a second, but she quickly masked it.

What the fuck was that about?

"Likewise," he greeted, accepting her handshake.

I didn't have to ask him if they knew each other, because I was sure they'd lie to my ass any damn way. Besides, why ask a question you already know the answer to?

My mind wandered to moments prior. *She lowered her*

gun before I could tell her Hollis was my brother. Hollis and Genesis had met before and not through me. From what I recalled, not at the wedding either.

They could have seen each other at the wedding though.

"You two met before?" I finally asked, unable to help myself.

"Nah," Hollis stated.

"Nope," Genesis followed after.

Having the Selena and Constantine connection was one thing. Discovering she had a friend that had gone missing was another. But my brother? What the fuck did he have to do with all this shit? Better yet, why weren't either of them owning up to it?

A ding on my phone had me glancing at the notification from Duchess that an emergency family meeting was needed. Hollis glanced at his phone, too, having received the same group message I did.

Did they fuck before? Genesis had been kind of blocked from his view by my body, but still. At the very least, I should have questioned Hollis right then and there, but something held me back. Maybe it was disappointment that the truth would affect me more than I'd ever admit. Or even that I questioned if I'd get the truth out of either of them.

However, as Genesis' phone dinged right after mine and Hollis', my curiosity was turning to anger and I didn't like that shit. "Aren't you gonna see who it is?"

She shrugged. "It's probably not important."

"Hmm, right." I noticed the defiant gleam in her eyes as she refused to look at it, her shoulders tense as if she were already preparing how to answer any questions I would shoot her way.

I didn't have to ask her shit though. My gut told me the message was from Duchess, so instead of going back and forth, I stated, "We'll pack up our shit and head back tomorrow morning so we can quit the bullshit and y'all can tell me what the fuck is going on."

No point in pretending. The shit was getting old real fast.

CHAPTER 10

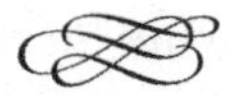

Fuck Dick, Worship Pussy

GENESIS

He was mad as hell, not that I could blame him. And he and I both knew damn well I had received a message from Duchess and needed to be on that flight back to Chicago.

It was weird because I'd kept secrets my entire life. Lying with ease if the situation called for it. In a lot of ways, it was necessary to protect my truth, but Pharaoh was one of the most honest men I knew despite that he had to lie sometimes because of what he did for a living. He was a sharpshooter. He didn't bullshit when it came to saying exactly how he felt.

Luckily, any questioning would have to wait until we

left Mexico because right after Duchess sent out the messages, Constantine let Pharaoh know that one of the men he suspected was behind the kidnapping of three women in Mexico two days ago—two locals and one tourist—was at Delilah.

Pharaoh hadn't wanted me to head to the strip club, but I insisted after finding out Selena was there.

"What the hell happened between you two?" Selena asked me once we entered through the private door at Delilah. "I thought for sure y'all would fuck and make up."

"Well, we fucked," I muttered. "And the rest is a long story. I tagged along because I don't want you out there by yourself, so I'm here to help."

"Help me how?"

I nodded toward the door that I assumed led to the main part of the club. "Is the guy out there?"

"You mean Jorge? Yeah, that son of a bitch and a few of his crew are here. Me and two others who joined Delilah for the sole purpose of bringing down men like him will give them a private show in about twenty minutes. From what I've heard from women who've danced for him before, you would think he likes all that dominant shit, but instead, he rather women to tie him up and crap." Selena glanced over her shoulder at Pharaoh, who was talking to Constantine. "So if you're thinking about being in that private room with me, think again. I was only around you and Patrón for thirty minutes at most and could tell there was something going on there."

I shrugged, not willing to go into the long ordeal about me and Pharaoh. However, I did decide to tell her, "I've worked at a strip club before. That's how I met Patrón. We need information, and I know how to help you get it. Doesn't matter what he thinks. I'm my own woman."

Selena nodded, looking slightly relieved that she'd have

an ally who she trusted in there with her. "Okay then. Let's figure out Constantine's plan."

We walked over, my eyes on Pharaoh when I announced, "I'll be giving the dance with Selena, so tell us how you want this to go."

"Uh." Constantine raised his eyebrows and looked to Pharaoh, who stood there observing me, his eyes intense and expression unreadable.

After realizing he wouldn't object, Constantine continued, "From what we know, Jorge likes to meet women and take them to a private condo he has in Playa del Carmen. He has one of those BSDM rooms and he makes sure he gets the woman nice and drugged before he even invites her over. After staking out the property, we noticed that some women enter, but they never leave the complex."

"Could be an underground exit," Pharaoh stated. "Maybe a tunnel he shuffles the women through. I know Jorge's MO, and if the price is right, he don't give a shit about giving up his allies."

Constantine nodded. "That's exactly what we're hoping for. The cartel faction that's protecting him only has his back because they went rouge after two of their superiors didn't see eye to eye. However, my sources tell me a lot of them ain't with the shit Jorge's superior pulls. They're still loyal, but if Selena can get him to bring her to his place, we're in."

"Who is his superior?" I asked.

"The wife of one of the most ruthless men I've ever met," Constantine replied.

Selena's eyes widened. "A woman?"

"Unfortunately, there are more and more women getting involved with human trafficking every year," I answered. "I lived in London for a little while and helped a friend of mine find a few missing Australian tourists. We were shocked that it was a woman who lured them to go with her by pretending to be a solo traveler. I researched it further and was surprised by the results."

I chanced a look at Pharaoh, not surprised to find his eyes glued to me. It wasn't the answer he wanted, but it was my way of offering an olive branch by sharing a small piece of my past with him.

"I get the feeling you've put yourself in danger more than a few times," he voiced.

"I would rather fight hard for my beliefs and die fighting, than live in a world where I turned a blind eye to what's wrong. Don't you agree?"

"You already know I do."

I wanted to kiss him right then and there. It wasn't any different than what I always wanted to do to him, but at the moment, a kiss seemed to be the next course of action after that admission, but we still had a plan to implement.

"Okay, so I have to appeal to Jorge enough to pique his interest," Selena stated, taking a deep breath. "I think I can do that."

"This shit could go sideways," I muttered out loud, although I had meant to only think it.

"It could," Pharaoh agreed. "And that's why I'll be in the room with you."

"Uh, um. How …" I scratched the back of my head, trying to find my words. "Do you think that's a good idea?"

Pharaoh's shit eating grin was undeniable. "I do. Jorge ain't stupid. He suspects that something is going down tonight, but he's always been too fuckin' curious to see what it is to stop it. That's why he's here at Delilah. So we'll play the game his way, but on our turf."

I nodded as they discussed how Selena and I would enter the room, deciding that Marie, a woman whose sister committed suicide after a terrible kidnapping ordeal, would assist in the show.

The ladies and I got ready fairly quickly and shared a supportive group hug, each of us emotional thinking about the physical and psychological abuse that human trafficking victims went through. There was never a day that went by where I wasn't in awe over how impressive and powerful women were. How our scars and tribulations only made us more resilient in this fucked up world.

We walked into the darkened room, a purplish pink glow that reminded me of the Delilah flower in its color. The room had several velvet chairs, but only three were stationed in front of two poles.

Jock, Hollis, and a few of Constantine's men were stationed throughout Delilah, keeping watch and making sure nothing popped off. Jorge had insisted that his first right hand get a front row seat to the show, and to be honest, we were just glad it wasn't the whole lot of them.

The laced lavender ensemble I was wearing left little to the imagination, instantly making me wish I was back in my twenty-something year old body where shit was still perky. Even so, the way Pharaoh was hungrily looking at me, his eyes roaming up and down my body, made me feel as if no time had passed between us since the first time he spotted me in his strip club.

Selena and I went to the same pole, Marie to the one on the end when the music started. As we began dancing, we knew the rules. Here in this room, they could touch as much as they wanted. Be as forward as they desired.

I was no stranger to the pole, having even taken classes to perfect my skills after I abruptly left Chicago fifteen years ago. In a way, I always felt like being on the pole connected me to Pharaoh despite the distance between us.

I never had time to watch television, but I stayed up on

my music, rolling my hips as my back remained planted against the side of the pole as "Wild Side" by Normani and Cardi B came on. I let the smooth beat take over, climbing to the top of the pole to show my moves before Selena slid right under me, both of us moving with ease against the cool steel in a way that made it seem like we did this shit every day.

Pharaoh's eyes weren't the only ones glued to us as I glanced over and caught Jorge unable to stop looking at myself or Selena. Marie was working her magic as well, the attention of Jorge's right hand solely on her.

The reason we were at Delilah was one none of us took lightly, but the energy was electric, my mind and my body consumed with wanting to put on a good show, while still maintaining focus.

From higher on the pole I was closer to one of the lights, so I couldn't make out Pharaoh's face. All I could see were his white Jordans and jean-clad legs open in a way that looked casual, but only made me want to sit on his dick.

I could see his watch, too; the gold Audemars Piguet glistening every time he lifted his wrist to take a sip of his premium Añejo drink. Even from the neck down, Pharaoh was my type in every way. Dangerous, with a good heart. Street smart, but even more intelligent than anyone realized. In a way, he defined what I wanted in a man all those years ago and I wasn't ashamed to admit that all the freaky shit we did was the best of my lifetime. I didn't just love sucking dick. I loved sucking *his* dick and that was a big fucking difference.

I'd never known a man who could fuck you without actually fucking you. That's what he did to me. That's how his kisses felt on my body. That's how much he knew what I liked without me saying shit. It was the way his eyes roamed over me with a scorching fire that could never be put out.

When I slid down the pole, it almost felt like I was unwrapping a gift as more of his face came into view with every second until those dark eyes met mine. I continued to dance, noticing Marie and Selena sharing a look before Marie came to our side and placed a soft peck on my lips.

Inwardly, I gasped in surprise, but I didn't show it. Couldn't show it under Jorge's scrutiny and obvious amusement.

I'd always been able to appreciate the beauty of a woman and how marvelously complex we were created. Yet, I didn't make it a habit of kissing girls and loved dick more than most, but oh the fuck well, I was into it with them. Their lips were soft … much softer than a man's. Selena had been vocal about her free sexuality since I'd met her, and it was clear that Marie and Selena weren't out of their comfort zone like I was. For whatever reason, both wanted to focus on me, each alternating pulling me in for a kiss as we danced together through another song, bodies moving in beautiful fluidity.

"Let's bring it home," Selena whispered so that only myself and Marie could hear. I absently nodded, too far in the moment to even know what I was agreeing to.

Selena and Marie both untied their lace bralettes at the same time before Selena bit her bottom lip and untied mine while Marie gripped my naked breasts. We were back to kissing and dancing, enjoying the moment for what it was.

I was more than sure Pharaoh had had his fair share of threesomes, but the way he was watching us—mainly me, though—was intoxicatingly addictive. His drink was forgotten, and he sat with his hands clasped, licking his lips at me in a way that had me moaning from thoughts of earlier in the villa.

We broke apart when "Thot Shit" by Megan Thee Stallion came through the speakers, the three of us sharing a look to execute the rest of the plan as we went into the lap dance portion of the night.

Any worry I'd briefly had about being rusty with my lap dances was shot to hell when I reached Pharaoh, both hips and ass bucking to the beat of the music. A part of me thought Pharaoh may just sit there and let me do my thang. However, the moment his hands touched my thighs when I straddled him, I lost it, thrashing my head back and rolling over the zipper of his jeans.

In my peripheral, I saw Marie get on her knees, obviously about to make Jorge's right hand man real fucking happy, while Selena was mounting Jorge in a twisted, sideways move that didn't even seem physically possible, restricting him in a way he liked.

"Making me hard as fuck wasn't part of the plan," Pharaoh whispered, pulling my head to his ear and kissing my tattoo in the process.

"Punish me for it," I taunted, sliding off his lap to shake my ass in his face, not giving a damn that my breasts were still exposed. It wasn't until I dropped my ass into his lap a few times, twerking to "WAP" by Cardi B and Megan Thee Stallion that Pharaoh tired of my antics and spun me around before slightly angling his chair away from the others and pulling me back into his lap.

"You play too fuckin' much," he huffed, pulling one of my breasts into his mouth, causing me to squeal.

"I don't play enough," I retorted, unzipping his jeans and pulling out his dick in a way that had him raising an eyebrow, but not saying shit else as he pulled my wet panties to the side, and I eased myself down over his dick.

"Shit," he groaned, both his hands finding my hips to help steady me as I bounced up and down in the chair, the legs skidding across the floor and making a rubbing noise.

Fucking Pharaoh at the strip club was *not* the original plan, but I dared any woman to look into his hypnotizing eyes, juicy lips, trimmed beard, and pull-me dreads and not want to throw her pussy at him. I was only human.

We were both enjoying the fuck out of this mission, but we also still noticed what was going on around us.

"Marie just took that dude back to the main room," Pharaoh muttered to me, his dick continuing to drive into my pussy.

"Uh huh." I nodded and moaned, noticing Jorge slip something into Selena's mouth as she sucked his finger, the act making me cringe knowing that his countdown to get her out of Delilah and to his place had started. "He planted the seed. You ready?"

"Bet."

I wasn't sure if I'd asked him if he was ready to come or ready to follow Jorge out of Delilah, but he answered both when he sucked my other breast, two fingers doing a gentle press and rotating rub against my clit, causing me to release an orgasm that made me want to scream out loud. Instead, I moaned into his mouth, moving my hips faster when he came right after, holding me securely in place as he did.

When he kissed him, I felt that kiss *everywhere*. We reluctantly broke apart, breathless and still intimately connected. "They're gone," he mentioned, indicating that Jorge had taken the bait, and him and Selena were headed to his place.

"I see."

His eyes studied mine. "Have you ever fucked Hollis?"

I shook my head. "Never have. Don't want to." I

suckled his bottom lip, my voice low when I whispered, "You're all I ever wanted. Your dick and your dick only."

He groaned and gripped the back of my head, running his hands between my braids as he kissed me again, hungrier than before, but just as tantalizing.

I could kiss his lips and ride his dick all damn night, but duty called and we were short on time. When the curtain to the door moved, Pharaoh stood and managed to shield us before they walked in.

"If y'all are done, we got some shit to handle," Constantine stated, popping his head in.

"Take Hollis with you and I'll follow with Jock and Genesis," Pharaoh told him.

"Okay."

Once we were alone, Pharaoh unbuttoned his shirt and placed it over me.

"Thanks."

"You're welcome." His eyes glinted with amusement. "That was unexpected."

I raised an eyebrow. "You complaining?"

"Fuck nah." He gripped my ass before giving it a light spank. "But I wasn't tryin' to fuck you again until we laid all our cards on the table."

I looked down at his dick that was now zipped back up, but still pressing on his jeans. "Well, apparently, he didn't get the memo."

His face grew serious. "We handle this shit, then we handle *our* shit."

I nodded. "We will." After all, I couldn't be a boss bitch in life, but clam up when it came to telling Pharaoh everything, even if that *everything* wasn't only my truth to tell.

* * *

PHARAOH

"So THAT'S what you all set this up for, huh?" Jorge asked an hour later. "You think I'm responsible for those missing women."

"Cut the shit," I told him. "You're above lyin' when you're caught, and you and I both know I can't stand a weak ass muthafucka who won't admit shit when he's been found out."

Jorge didn't drop the smirk on his face as he looked from me to Constantine. Genesis, Jock, and I arrived at the complex a couple minutes after the others, and Constantine and his guys were already inside. Hollis had been waiting for us on the outside.

When Jorge realized his men didn't want to fight Constantine's men and make enemies of a cartel group larger than their rebel crew, they stood down. Something was telling me Jorge hadn't wanted a fight anyway. I'd seen him around for years, our paths crossing here and there, but he didn't seem as carefree as he had in the past. It looked like the years had taken their toll.

"It's true," he finally admitted. "Those women did disappear here at my complex, but one of my men knew they were a target and we brought them here for protection. My boss gets a bad rep, but we broke ties with the others because we didn't like how they do business."

"So you're saying you didn't sell them?" I asked.

"No, I didn't." He raised his hands. "I'm gonna pull out a map, that's all."

Constantine and I still had our pistols pointed at him just in case. Jorge had his men in the room like we had ours, but to be honest, everything felt as civil as it could be.

"We have been offering women a safe place to live if we get wind that they are being targeted. If they are a tourist, we make sure they get safely out of the country." Jorge glanced over my shoulder at Selena and Genesis before looking to Constantine. "One of my men told me what he suspected as the true goal of Delilah and that he thought we should align together."

"You could have asked me for a fucking meeting," Constantine said. "Instead, you pretended to be on some other shit."

Jorge shrugged. "I had more fun this way."

"What did you give me then?" Selena asked. "When you slipped something into my mouth."

"A sugar pill," he explained. "It keeps up appearances if others think I got to their target first. Plus, it's all about convincing the mind. Doesn't matter if it isn't the real shit." He winked at Selena, to which she spat a slew of Spanish curse words his way.

"Why should we believe you're telling us the truth?" Constantine asked.

"This shit is personal for you," I answered, speculating.

"It is," he confirmed. "I guess you could say I fell for a woman who was meant to be someone else's captive and the shit didn't end well."

"I'm sorry," Selena said, softening a bit. "That sucks."

"Thanks." This time, when Jorge smiled at Selena, it was different. Sincere. I still didn't trust the muthafucka, but it was better to have more for the cause than against it.

"I wanna help," he stated, on cue. "However my men and I can assist, we will."

Constantine and I looked at each other, silently communicating in a way one could with friends they trusted in our line of work.

We still had to figure out Jorge's role in all this, but tonight had gone well. Regardless, it was clear that we needed to be better at hiding our motive and goal for the strip clubs and app. Otherwise, the shit wouldn't work.

And Genesis remains to be a big fucking problem. I couldn't believe after all this time, I was still in love with a woman with too many damn secrets. That much was obvious. She'd been my Ginx then. My unlucky charm since fucked up shit seemed to happen when we were together. And just like all those years ago, a muthafucka like me would get hurt again if I wasn't careful.

CHAPTER 11

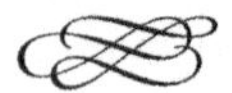

Fuck Secrets, Get Answers

PHARAOH

Hollis and Genesis didn't say shit in the jet that I reserved to take us back to Chicago. As a matter of fact, Hollis hadn't said much to me since he found us on the balcony. Hell, I'd enlisted Jock's help to make sure that fool didn't marry Yasmine's gold-digging ass. I'd been there. Done that. Had the child support receipts to prove it.

"Any idea on when Duchess and Stan are arriving?" Keaton asked. "I have a date tonight."

"With who?" Korie inquired. "I thought you broke up with that professor from Loyola University."

"I did," she explained. "But I'm dating this other

professor now. He teaches at Northwestern and he's fine as hell."

Taraj laughed. "What is it with you and professors? He's like the fourth one you've dated in the past year."

Keaton shrugged. "I don't know. I guess I just get tired of dating men who I may end up representing in court." She looked to the side of the room where me, Saint, Jedidiah, Hollis, and Creed were standing. "No offense, fam."

"None taken," Jackie D replied.

My ex-wives had never been invited to family meetings, but my brothers' partners were different. More loyal and trustworthy than my exes had ever been and understanding of the life we lived. As I listened to the women talk, my eyes drifted to Creed as they often did in moments that reminded me of Tristan. I'd never seen a couple more in love than them, and although my brother was *slowly* starting to heal, he wasn't the same and probably never would be.

Genesis isn't here either. I was pretty damn sure someone in my family had been messaging her back in Mexico, but when I asked, of course she denied it, claiming she had to get home for something Noble had going on. Noble hadn't answered my call when I reached out to pick his brain about it.

"Hellooooo, family," Nash boasted, earning my attention as he walked into the grand room with Jade shaking her head beside him. "I hope y'all didn't miss us too much while we were in the Maldives on our honeymoon."

"Hey, what did y'all bring me?" Hollis asked, already looking through the beach bag on Jade's shoulder.

Jade smacked his hand away. "Boy, you betta stop digging in my bag like you're a fucking child."

He frowned. "So you ain't bring me shit?"

Rolling her eyes, she dug around until she pulled out a box of cigars. "Here. They are top notch and expensive as hell, so don't smoke them all in one night."

"That's what I'm talkin' 'bout." He pulled her into a hug before saluting Nash and returning to the chair he'd vacated.

"You're right on time," Saint told them. "Duchess and Stan aren't here yet."

"Any idea what this is about?" Nash asked.

All eyes turned to me since I was usually the one who knew what was going on first. To be honest, it wasn't sitting right with me being in the dark like this, but shit was shifting in this family. In what ways, I wasn't sure.

"They didn't say," I answered.

Nash's eyes widened. "Get the fuck outta here. You tellin' me you don't know what's going on?"

"I don't." My eyes drifted to Hollis who could put on a poker face with his frenemies, but was transparent as hell with his family. "Any clue what's going on, Hollis?"

"Hollis?" Saint looked from me to him. "Why would he know?"

"I don't know anything," he answered, giving me a stern look before he became completely engrossed in his cigars.

Creed caught my gaze, his eyes squinting in observance at the awkward exchange between Hollis and me.

"Y'all good?" Jedidiah asked, apparently witnessing the same thing. "Or did something happen in Mexico y'all need to get off your chest?"

We didn't get a chance to answer as Duchess and Stan walked into the room, with Queenie rolling in in her wheelchair right after. However, it was the two teenagers straggling in behind them that had all our attention.

"Gather around," Duchess requested, each of us moving from our respective corners of the room to gather at the elongated wooden table that they'd installed as the family continued to grow.

"I'm sure you're all wondering why we called you here today," Stan stated, motioning for the teenagers to stand beside them. "There's no easy way to ease into this, so I'll let someone else explain it better."

To my surprise, Creed—who had been standing beside me—stood and walked over to the kids, hugging them both and kissing their foreheads, the embrace one that I knew all too well. The boy and girl appeared to be around thirteen or fourteen years old, both looking like a mix between Creed and Tristan.

"You're a father," I muttered, thinking back to years ago when I'd suspected Tristan was pregnant before she disappeared for a while.

"I am," Creed confirmed, looping an arm over each of his kids. "Family, this is Christian and Trinity, mine and Tristan's twins."

My siblings began whispering in the room, each of them surprised … except Hollis. "You knew about them?"

"Not at first," he answered. "But yes, I learned of their existence a year ago."

"How could I not know this?" Nash asked.

"We wanted it that way," Creed answered. "I've done some things in my past I'm not proud of. Made enemies with the wrong people. I know most of us in this room have, but for their safety, we wanted to keep them away from Chicago and a possible target on their backs. Especially from Tristan's parents. We sent them off to boarding school, but for the holiday's and breaks, they usually stay with Micah Madden, Carter's brother. Micah has been taking them to a safe house to see us for the past six years. In our family, only Duchess and Stan knew of their existence."

"But we know all about each of you," Christian stated, wearing a smile, whereas Trinity still seemed a little more reserved. "Our parents made sure we knew where we came from." Christian looked to Creed, his eyes watery and full of emotion by the time he turned back to us. "Trinity and I want to thank you for loving our mother. She talked about you guys all the time, during every visit, phone conversation, and letter."

"I can't believe she was a mom," Taraj muttered, dabbing the corners of her eyes as Saint leaned over and squeezed her shoulders. "She was the sister I always wanted."

"She knew it," Christian told her. "She told me Auntie Taj would be the first to buy us liquor for our sixteenth birthday."

"Um, nah," she said, laughing. "Maybe eighteen at best."

Christian smiled. "Fair enough." Christian nodded to Hollis. "Uncle Henny gave us the lowdown on everything our parents didn't want us to know."

Hollis smiled. "Just doing my job early to hopefully win the title of favorite uncle."

Trinity laughed for the first time since entering the room, her eyes landing on Keaton. "According to Mom, I'm a lot like you. I love to debate, and she always said if I wanted to learn more about being a lawyer, you were the woman to talk to."

"Anytime you need me, sweetie," Keaton mentioned, walking over to hug Trinity and Christian, which started a chain reaction around the room.

"Uncle Saint and Jackie D!" Christian dabbed fists with them both. "She called you the protectors of the family. The ones to call no matter what the problem and you'd be there, no questions asked."

"You've always got us," Saint stated.

"Just say the word," Jackie D added.

When their eyes landed on Korie, Trinity's eyes widened, and Christian cleared his throat.

"Sorry," he said. "It's just … you remind us of her."

"It's in your eyes," Trinity revealed.

"You knew about me?" Korie asked, wiping the corners of her eyes as she hugged them both.

Christian nodded. "We did."

I was sure he was going to say more, but Korie pulled them in for another hug and it wasn't lost on me that through them, she would get to know another side of her sister she never had the privilege to see.

Hollis finally cracked a joke about Korie suffocating them and she let them go, but not before squeezing in another quick hug.

"We heard you'd never settle down," Christian said to Nash before hugging Jade. "Glad you came to your senses."

Jade beamed. "So smart, this niece and nephew of mine."

"How old are you again?" Nash asked.

"Fourteen," they said in unison.

"Fourteen going on forty I see." He was feigning like he was annoyed, but was smiling ear to ear.

When I finally reached them, I was surprised how much emotion I felt. Tristan and I were always close, but then again, everyone had felt that way about her. "I feel her spirit in you both," I told them. "Hers and Creed's."

As I pulled the twins to me, I looked over their heads at Creed who, on the outside, seemed to be holding it together, but I knew more than the others that seeing his children with all us was something he'd imagined ten times over. He gave me a quick smile, and honestly, it was more than I could ask for with the emotions I was sure were coursing through his body.

"Mom always said you were the glue," Christian disclosed, Trinity nodding along with him. "To her, you were the ultimate big brother. Never bothering the family with your burdens and taking care of everyone else before yourself."

His words hit me in the heart. "Tris always did see me as a much better man than I am."

"You legally adopted five kids in addition to your own because you wanted them to have a better life," Trinity disclosed. "She admired you for that so much."

"Is that true?" Hollis asked.

I shrugged. "It's not important." Why I'd shared that information with Tristan, I wasn't sure. She had just been that kind of person. You wanted to open up to her. When she smiled with pride, you felt like you did something right.

"I just assumed when you introduced the kids of your exes as yours, that you actually fathered them," Hollis added.

"If I told you they're mine, then I am their father," I corrected.

"I didn't know that," Nash said, guilt in his eyes. "Why didn't you say anything when we constantly teased you about having so many kids?"

"Because it's true. Doesn't matter if they blood or not. If at one point in their life I became their guardian, they're mine even if I'm not with their mom. Especially if I can make their life better than the circumstances they were born into."

"I always suspected something like that," Saint admitted, prideful eyes staring back at me.

"I'm sure a few of you have," I divulged. "As close as we all are, there will always be something to discover about each other. Secrets we keep private for one reason or another. Yet, in our family, loyalty and trust are the pillars we are built on. Blood didn't make us family, but heart and dedication did. I want that for my future and my kids' future. I want them to realize that if they are the kids of Pharaoh Pierce Crowne, that's not a temporary arrangement and I love them all the same."

The room settled into a comfortable silence, my siblings looking at me in an admirable way they hadn't in a long time. I never needed to be the protector like Saint and Jedidiah, or the comic relief like Hollis. I wasn't the business savvy brother like Nash, and I couldn't seek justice for those wronged quite like Keaton could. We hadn't seen Doc in years, but Doc and Creed always had this special something that made others listen when they spoke. When they said something, you knew they meant it.

For me, being in the streets was where I shone best. People followed my lead and in return, I took care of them. My loyalty was with the Crownes, but family for me was beyond that. Even beyond my kids, Jock, and my blood relatives. Or friends like Cash, Keon, and Niko.

It stemmed to those I met along my journey who managed to impact my life like I did theirs. I loved hard. Always had. My siblings knowing no matter where they are in the world, I'll be in Chicago holding things down has always been something I take seriously. I didn't just push drugs or run strip clubs, and despite them knowing the ultimate goal behind some of my decisions, I'd never apologize for doing what I love. I was born for this life.

In a way, we categorized each other based off the role we had in the family … yet, it took meeting my latest niece and nephew for me to open up during a family meeting in a way I never had before. To show my siblings a side of myself I didn't share because it never seemed as important as the shit they had going on.

I'm not sure what made me look up at the door that was cracked open, but I did, spotting the one person I'd expected to pop up tonight and another I didn't understand was there at all, but still glad to see.

Noble walked my way first, the silence in the room still heavy from my prior words. He hugged me, whispering, "Go easy on her," before stepping back and standing beside Christian and Trinity.

Genesis hugged me next, composed on the outside, but I felt the tension in her shoulders.

"What's going on?" I asked, leaning back from our embrace to look into her eyes.

Her smile was genuine, but laced in apprehension. "You're finally getting the rest of those answers you've wanted for years." Instead of staying by my side, she stood on the other side of Stan, my mind even more confused on what the fuck was going on.

"Let me start by saying, I owe you an apology," Duchess stated, looking solely at me.

I didn't glance around at my siblings' faces, but Duchess didn't do apologies or accept them either. She expected us to do better if we fucked up, and in exchange, we placed that same expectation on her and Stan.

Therefore, if Duchess was apologizing before even telling me the reason, the best thing I could do was keep my emotions in check off bat.

"Fifteen years ago, I discovered that Genesis was pregnant with your child," Duchess explained, prompting me to cross my arms over my chest in a defensive pose.

"I've been wondering what you were hiding since Genesis returned," I admitted, my tone accusatory.

"I suspected early on that Genesis was Esi's daughter and that Booker was her brother even though I hadn't seen Genesis since she was a young girl," Duchess explained. "I've known Noble Senior for a long time, and if Genesis was working under the guise of a stripper, it was for one reason and one reason only."

"I didn't know right away, but I learned later that she had infiltrated my life to kill me for retribution for Booker," I admitted, looking from Genesis to Noble who wore the same stoic expression as his mother.

"It was more than that," Duchess disclosed, glancing to Stan before addressing my siblings. "I know all of you have wondered for quite some time the business Stan and I handle while we're away, and all we ask is that you listen with an open mind."

Duchess nodded at Genesis who took a deep breath, her eyes holding mine hostage when she said, "The first time I met Duchess, I was a little girl and she saved me from an overseas prison camp for kids."

"Prison camps don't still exist, right?" Hollis asked, surprising me by not already knowing what would come out of Genesis' mouth considering he seemed to know other shit he wasn't letting on.

"They do," Genesis said. "For obvious reasons, they aren't widely known, but I was kept at a location with other illegitimate children of leaders of European organized crime. Esi is my mother, but my stepdad, Noble, isn't my biological father."

"And Booker wasn't your biological brother," I pointed out. "Why didn't you tell me?"

I couldn't read the expression on her face. "He was my family in all the ways that mattered. I admit that mentally, he began to lose himself, and I think knowing you before you were adopted by Duchess and Stan just ate away at him because he watched you transform into the kind of man he wanted to be. Jealousy can eat away at even the sanest mind, but Booker was still my family, and before I even met you, I was angry at what you took away from Noble Senior, the first man to show me real kindness. He needed retribution, and I knew I could offer that to him … Meeting you just got more complicated than that."

"Esi had thought Genesis was dead," Duchess explained. "When she got wind her daughter hadn't died after she'd given birth, we did what we could to find her."

"The man who fathered me didn't make it easy," Genesis explained, looking around the room again. "Igor Popov was my father, and was the leader of the Bratva residing in Chicago. In the Bratva, children of two Russian parents were treated like precious thoroughbreds to the mafia crown, whereas, even the hint of something different in your blood deems you unfit to call yourself a Russian. At least that's how it was in old school Russia. As one of the biggest drug trafficking cities in the States, you can imagine why he didn't want anyone, including my mother, to know about me."

"Sorry for what happened to your father," Korie mentioned, referring to Igor.

"No apology needed," she said, looking between Jedidiah and Korie. "I'd like to think he cared for my mom as she did him when they were younger, but Igor was known for seducing women just to bed them and leave. My mother could have been no different. She wanted me to know where I came from, but not forget that they robbed me of my childhood."

"And that's why you wanted to work together to bring down Boris," I implied. "Your half-brother who was trained to take over Igor's empire is taking what's rightfully yours."

"I don't want any ties with the Popovs," she claimed. "They aren't my family in any of the ways that matter. However, Boris found out about me, and in his mind, I shouldn't have lived at all, let alone bore a child." She closed her eyes tightly before opening them again. "Boris took my mother to force me to face him. I'm not sure if she's even alive, but I need to find her if she is. He always thought Igor was too weak, so I doubt he misses his father. All of this is a ploy to ensure that illegitimate or not, I never come for what he believes is rightfully his. Things are changing in Russia and everything isn't so black and white as it was when I was born."

"We need to find Boris," Jedidiah stated. "I didn't pinpoint why he was waiting to strike, but it makes sense that he's trying to sniff you out of Chicago."

"We know where Boris is," Christian stated.

"He's living underground, below the Chicago pedway tunnels," Trinity supplied.

"He's been hiding down there for a while," Noble added, my eyes observing how close the three seemed and witnessing the looks of pride on Creed and Genesis' faces. "We were able to track some of his crew by putting on fake school uniforms we purchased and pretending to walk home from school every time we tracked them."

Trinity pulled out a piece of paper from her pocket and handed it to Genesis. "I just finished composing the schedule on our way over. I detailed the times they eat, get supplies, track all of you." She glanced around the room. "It's not perfect, but it'll help."

"How do y'all know how to do all this?" Saint asked. "Instinct?"

Christian, Trinity, and Noble settled their eyes on Duchess.

"It's been happening this whole time, hasn't it?" I asked, looking to Stan and Duchess. "You started the academy."

Duchess nodded. "We did. You're looking at Couronne d'Ombre Academy's three longest attending students who enrolled at the start."

"I don't understand," Keaton stated. "This is a school for what exactly?"

"For people like us," Duchess proclaimed. "You all are aware how much I despise the negative connotation the word *criminal* holds. Couronne d'Ombre stands for Shadow Crown, and in the academy, we hone the skills and traits that make criminals great at what we do starting them young and encouraging the next generation to be smarter, better, and more adaptable to the world they were born in."

"Before high school, students have the option to attend full-time since the school isn't located in the States," Stan explained next. "When they reach their freshman year of high school, studies increase and we request our students be on campus throughout the year with holiday breaks in between. By college, education is enhanced to an even higher hands-on learning experience."

"I've never heard of anything like that before," Taraj stated, holding her stomach and smiling up at Saint like they were already certain their unborn child would be attending.

"So Creed and Tristan made the decision to enroll

their kids in this academy you and Stan started, but I was robbed of the opportunity to decide where my son spent the early part of his life?" My voice was slightly raising, but I didn't give a fuck.

"The birth of the twins and Noble is what encouraged Stan and I to finally turn our dream into a reality," Duchess justified.

"Which still included me being in the dark."

"Can't you tell it's more complicated than that?" Genesis asked.

"I can tell a lot of shit that I didn't recognize before."

She flinched, but didn't say more.

"I know you're upset," Duchess stated. "And I understand why you're angry."

"Nah, you don't." I looked from her to Genesis. "You had every moment to tell me the truth, and yet, I find out this shit when everyone else finds out even though one of my fuckin' kids goes to the damn school."

It used to be rare that I got pissed, but lately, keeping my anger in check was difficult. When I lost my cool, my siblings knew to shut the fuck up.

"We can talk after this," Genesis said, exhaustion evident in her facial features. "I hate that you're finding all this out this way, but we can't hold out on Boris anymore. My contact tells me he's planning something big, and we need to strike first."

"Two nights from now," Duchess confirmed.

As everyone began spouting questions and ideas of attack left to right, I stood back and focused on controlling how angry I felt. *Not angry, betrayed.* If there was one thing I knew about how Duchess and Stan operated, it was that everything had a reason and there was a reason for everything.

They owed me an explanation, and despite everything

Genesis had revealed, I still needed clarification on some things. I had a right to be pissed, and despite how impressed I was with Noble and the twins, the fact that Creed and Hollis never whispered a word of any of this to me was another betrayal.

I trusted the people in this room with my life, but right now, my disappointment was overpowering my ability to focus on the importance of the situation.

CHAPTER 12

Fuck Family, Do You

PHARAOH

"Glad we found you here," Creed stated, stepping past the door of my home, Hollis, Saint, Jedidiah, and Nash following behind him.

"I almost let y'all asses stay outside."

"We know last night was a lot for you." Saint sat down across from me in my living room where I'd been doing nothing but sipping bourdon and staring at the wall. "When none of us heard from you today, we figured we should stop by."

"I didn't have shit to say today," I admitted. "Was still processing." My eyes landed on Creed and Hollis. "Did either of you ever think to tell me what you knew?"

"The moment I met Noble I did," Creed answered. "I met him as a young boy, but before this summer, I didn't know Genesis like that even though our paths crossed at times. You know more than anyone that when Duchess has a plan, no one can stop her from fulfilling it. Tris and I went back and forth on what to do to keep the twins safe. When we confided in Duchess and Stan, informing them that we wanted to keep the twins away from the life we lived, they informed us about the school we never knew existed. I was against sending them away, but Tris insisted that regular boarding school would never work for kids who would bear the last name Crowne. She wanted them to be better at living in our world than she had been. Smarter at recognizing a friend versus foe and aware of the history of mafia families no matter what their race or nationality. They learn that at the academy."

"If you think about it, the school actually began with us over thirty years ago," Hollis pointed out. "They weren't calling it Couronne d'Ombre then, but a few of us suspected this was something Duchess and Stan had always intended to do."

"That's true," I stated. "Used to have my ass fallin' asleep during lessons."

"That's because they kept us in classes ten hours a day minimum," Jedidiah reminded.

Saint nodded. "And all of us used to wonder how life would have been if we'd been more informed at a younger age."

"The only reason I found out about the academy last year was because of Tristan's death," Hollis explained. "We needed to know our enemies, and Duchess and Stan requested I look into every avenue, including teachers and staff at the academy."

"Tris taught at the school on occasion," Creed

explained. "It was a way for her to stay close to the kids and educate as well since teaching was always her passion."

"And I almost closed the academy down after her death," Duchess stated, walking into the room with the slyness of a cat.

I took another sip of my bourbon. "I didn't know you were here."

"I used my key." She sat in the only vacant seat. "I just wanted to make sure you were okay."

"Did you tell Genesis to stop seeing me years ago?"

She nodded. "I did, but it was for your own good."

"How?"

"Back then, you couldn't afford to make an enemy of the Russians, and that's exactly what you would have done if you'd married Igor's daughter. Your life wasn't private, and it still isn't, but you've found a balance. Plus, Esi and I both knew the complications that came from her stepson, Booker's, death and you needing the Black community who supported him to support you. Word got around fast that Genesis tried to kill you and those who were unsure of whether to follow you or not would have jumped ship. It was all too much. But I promise you, I didn't know she was pregnant until after Noble was born."

I took another sip of my drink, remembering a time when my status in the city had been on shakier grounds. "Even if I understood all that, why was Noble enrolled in the academy without me knowing of his existence? I could have kept his identity a secret just like Creed did for his children."

"It was different with you," Duchess stated. "We've never discussed this before, but right now, you have two sons and a daughter who want to take over your place in the city when you retire. Yet, you haven't chosen your successor, and although I love the father you are to your children, in our world, we need to groom a Crowne who would be able to infiltrate drug trafficking—amongst other things—throughout the world without many ties to this city."

"You needed to raise a soldier," I stated.

"Not a soldier," she corrected. "A warrior to bring down the unjust enemies that make this society unapologetically violent, especially for the black and brown. An individual with strong bloodlines on all sides, a heart made of steel, yet still empathetic when necessary, and one with unmatched intelligence. You were a Pierce before you were a Crowne. Genesis is a Popov and stems from a long line of Ghanaian warriors. Stan and I were able to teach you kids how to perfect your skills and crafts, yet with the academy, we were blessed to get some started at an earlier age. Noble, Christian, and Trinity are three of our best. Cousins, and the fiercest of allies." She reached over and gently touched the top of my hand. "Pharaoh, I will never know if not telling you was the right decision, but I can promise you that not a day went by where that boy didn't know how amazing his father is. Genesis has also been an extremely big help with the academy."

"How so?" I asked.

"Her journey hasn't been easy and she's in a unique position to offer insight on being a part of several different families, while also working for some of the secret intelligence organizations her mother, Esi, worked for. It's our goal to help the variety of mafias in the world understand each other better. Within her first few years of helping us, we successfully shut down the prison camp she'd been held hostage at. There are still more out there, but Genesis and others work actively to make large strides in eliminating these camps daily."

I couldn't help but smile at that. "She's always been special, so I'm not surprised to hear about her success."

"I'm ashamed to admit I didn't know how extraordinary she was until years after you realized her worth."

The sincerity in her voice gave me pause. Duchess wasn't the type to show emotion. I'd always been acutely aware of how hard it had to be for her to be so tough when every man you came into contact with looked to expose your weaknesses. For that reason, Duchess had always been tougher on women she worked with, knowing they had to fight harder to even be provided the opportunities a weak man were handed.

"I appreciate you explaining everything and I'll be fine," I said, not only to her, but to my brothers as well. "I'm just wrapping my head around it all."

"I hope you know that I really am sorry," Duchess stated, her eyes full of concern as she looked from me to Creed.

"What is it?" I asked, sensing she had more on her mind.

"Nothing," she said, much too quickly for her. "I mean, nothing we can't discuss later."

The room was much less tense once I got out of my feelings, until we got a call from Keaton telling us she heard from a client that Carla Jean was back in town. We left my place immediately, called Keaton and Korie to meet us there, and arrived at Carla Jean's old house only to find it empty.

"Somebody's fucking with us," Hollis stated, kicking at the dirt in the backyard.

"She really was here." Keaton walked from the side of the house with a note in her hand. "Or someone wants us to think she was."

"What does it say?" I asked.

"I didn't do it," Keaton read. "I didn't call a hit on my daughter." She flipped over the piece of paper. "That's it. Nothing else."

"Nah, there's something else," Jedidiah claimed, standing by the tall Emerald Green Arborvitae trees in the corner of the yard. My gut told me what it was before I even walked over.

"Damn," I huffed, all of us looking at Carla Jean's dead body.

Korie's hands flew to her face. "Why would she leave us that note and then kill herself?"

"She didn't," I stated, turning on the light on my phone so we could get a better look. "Notice the angle and color of her body. The foam at her mouth. The glazed whiteness in her eyes. Someone wanted this to look like an overdose."

"How can you be sure she didn't overdose?" Korie asked.

"Carla Jean hated the Crownes and everything we stood for," Duchess explained. "She'd never do drugs, let alone overdose."

"Do you think her husband did it?" Korie asked.

"Maybe." I glanced around at the same time Jedidiah did. "We need to bring her body back to the estate and get the hell outta here."

"My sentiments exactly," Jedidiah agreed.

Saint nodded. "I'll get my cleaning supplies from the truck."

When we got back to the house, Figgy and Saint got to work on analyzing Carla Jean's body, confirming what we'd already suspected. She'd been murdered. We didn't know why or by who, but it didn't sit right with any of us.

Unfortunately, all that would have to wait until we dealt

with Boris. It wasn't until I left to go see Genesis that I realized Creed hadn't said shit since we arrived at Carla Jean's house to find it empty.

An angry Creed was reckless.

A quiet Creed was someone else to fear entirely. When he got quiet, he was liable to fuck some shit up. Not now. Maybe not soon. Eventually though.

* * *

GENESIS

"AFTER THE NIGHT I HAD, the only person I wanted to see is you," he said. "Is it okay if I come in?"

I stood frozen at the door, surprised to see Pharaoh standing on the other side, his dreads falling around his head. He looked like he hadn't gotten much sleep yesterday, but still just as sexy in that just rolled out of bed kind of look.

"Duchess gave me your address," he explained.

Noble pulled open the door when I still didn't move. "Oh, hey, Dad. You can come in."

Pharaoh smiled, pulling Noble to him for a hug.

"Did I miss something?" Noble asked, his voice slightly muffled since his face was buried in Pharaoh's chest.

"You called me Dad," he explained, finally letting him go.

Noble shrugged. "I've known you were my dad my entire life. I know last night was overwhelming, but you're the most adaptable OG I know if all the stories I've heard about you and what I've learned myself is true."

Pharaoh shook his head. "You stay sayin' some slick shit."

Noble lifted an eyebrow. "You mean I'm always callin'

you on your shit and you ain't expect that from your younger, better looking son." He popped the top of his T-shirt.

"What did I tell you about cursing?" I asked, finally finding my voice.

"Ma, I'm practically grown."

"But you're not," I told him. "Now head to your room so me and your father can talk."

"Sure." He turned to Pharaoh, an elated expression on his face. "For what it's worth, I've looked up to you my entire life. Just because you ain't know it don't make it not true."

The prideful gleam in Pharaoh's eyes warmed my heart, his voice sounding a little choked up when he said, "I appreciate that, man."

Once we were alone, my nerves took full control, resulting in the only words I could spit out being, "Are you parched? I mean, ah, are you thirsty?" The words came out slightly throaty, sort of dreamy. Neither what I was aiming for, but both were better than squeaky.

Pharaoh's eyes darkened.

"For a drink," I clarified. "Cold beverage of choice."

"I'm good," he responded, smirking before he glanced around my place as he stepped farther inside. "It's been a long night."

"What happened?" I asked.

"I'll tell you later," he promised. "And I can get a tour later too, but there's something else I have to get off my chest first."

"I'm sure you do." I sighed, ready for him to start shooting out questions. I'm not sure what I thought those questions would be, but bracing myself did nothing to prepare me for the fact that words weren't on his mind as he pulled me into his arms and gripped the back of my braids that were secured in a ponytail holder.

"Hmm." My moan was immediate, his lips tasting like bourbon and his unique flavor that I'd always been addicted to. I welcomed the taste, my arms wrapping around his neck, clinging to him in a way that had me forgetting all my worries and anxiety from revelations of the night before.

"I'm sorry I didn't tell you all of this sooner," I muttered between kisses. "I just … nothing happened as I had planned."

His tongue coaxed mine a few more times in slow strokes before he broke the kiss and leaned his forehead to mine.

"You ain't alone in all this shit now that I know everything," he said, his hands grazing my cheeks and neck. "Tomorrow night, we kill Boris and find answers about your mom."

"We can't kill him yet, but if we don't capture him, I need to know that Noble is safe," I told him, my eyes pleading with his. "Meaning, if this shit goes sideways, I hope you know that I'll let Boris kill me if it means protecting those I care about. I'm the one he wants. Everyone else is just a casualty."

"It won't come to that, Ginx. I lost you once, and I understand now that you thought you were protecting me. I get why Noble had to go on this journey without me in his life. I've been thinking about my future a lot lately. My kids' future. What legacy I want to leave behind for them." He gently kissed my lips again, before pulling my bottom lip slightly, only letting go to continue saying, "I've been at this shit for so long, I ain't let myself think about what life after this would look like until you came back in my life. That night you tried to kill me, that fiery look you had in your eyes, I had never let an unexpected enemy get so close. I was torn between wanting to fuck you again and ignore what we both knew you were trying to do or demand answers. Looking back, I was willing to jeopardize shit I'd spent my whole life building for you."

"That's why I couldn't stay," I acknowledged. "Between my birth father and stepfather, the feelings we had for each other were muddied in my mind. Add to that, working for different private organizations to expose secret prison camps and being off the grid at times, I wasn't in the position to be anybody's life partner. I knew being with me was a risk you couldn't take, but damn, did I want to jeopardize it all to be with you."

His eyes studied mine. "We have now."

"And I promise you, no more secrets," I told him.

"Good." His hands gripped my ass tight. "'Cause I'm pretty fuckin' sure I ain't stopped lovin' yo' ass after all this time."

I smiled, my heart flip flopping at his words. "Turns out, I still love your muthafuckin' ass, too." This time, when he kissed me, I couldn't stop the moans from escaping my mouth. Shit was far from uncomplicated, but for right now, it felt as close to perfect as it could be under the circumstances.

Neither of us had remembered we weren't in the house alone until I heard keys rattling.

"Uh, Noble, where are you going?" I asked, stepping back from Pharaoh and smoothing out the front of my disheveled shirt.

"To the movies with Kennedy."

I glanced at my Apple watch. "It's almost midnight. There aren't any shows playing this late."

He muttered something under his breath. "Okay, so maybe we ain't going to the movies." Noble looked from

Pharaoh to me, smirking. "Summer break is almost over, though, and I'll have to go back to school."

"Kennedy is attending Couronne d'Ombre, so you'll see her plenty this school year."

"Ma, we don't get privacy like that at school," he complained. "Christian and Trinity are hanging out tonight, too. And Uncle Creed already got security trailing us like usual."

"Damn," Pharaoh huffed. "Creed told me the twins usually spend their summers with Carter's family, but knowing all our kids hang out and shit is still fuckin' wit' me."

I rolled my eyes, not even reminding him that yet again, he was still cursing in front of Noble freely. Obviously, Pharaoh ain't change for his kids, and honestly, I wasn't even sure I wanted him to.

"If you want, I can stay here and pretend not to hear y'all have sex, which clearly, is about to happen." Noble made a gagging sound. "I'm mature for my age, but no kid wants to hear that mess."

Before I could tell him wasn't nobody having sex tonight, Pharaoh pulled out a wad of cash from his pocket and clasped it into Noble's hand, bidding him a quick, "Have fun. Be safe. And don't do any shit that will piss Kennedy's father off."

Noble nodded. "Understood."

"Good. Don't come back for at least an hour."

"All you need is an hour?" Noble teased. "Why I got so many siblings if you only giving women one good hour? I guess king of the streets ain't king in the sheets, huh?"

"Boy, get the fuck outta here." Pharaoh practically pushed him out of the door, locking it as if Noble didn't have a key if he really wanted to come back in.

I was still laughing when Pharaoh turned my way until

I saw the expression on his face, ceasing my laughs. He leaned against the closed door, pure lust reflected in his eyes.

"I meant to tell you," I babbled, getting nervous out of nowhere, "the fact that you took legal guardianship or adopted so many kids that weren't yours is truly admirable. I heard you when Noble and I were waiting in the hallway at the estate. I'm not at all surprised because I know your heart."

"Thank you, but I don't take care of others for accolades."

"I know you don't," I told him. "I'm just impressed, and it made me love you that much more."

His shameless eyes stayed on mine, hinting at a night to remember. "You always know I craved to do that, huh, Ginx?"

I squinted. "Do what?"

"Impress you." He stepped closer to me. So close, I could barely look up at him without my nose brushing against his body. "Lead us to the bedroom," he directed.

I nodded like a damn bobble head and tried not to skip as I made my way down the hallway, anticipating what the night would bring. By the time I reached my bedroom and went to turn on another lamp in addition to the one that was already on, Pharaoh placed his hand over mine, halting me.

"Get naked and sit on the bed."

I did as told, slowly stripping my clothes, my eyes following his every move as he focused on what I was doing, while also lighting the four candles I had stationed around the room.

His large frame moved about the space like he'd been in my room before, prompting me to ask him just that out of curiosity.

"You used to talk about candles all the time," he answered. "I've never been here before, but I know you and to know you is to recognize details others may not realize."

When he took out his phone and began playing an Ella Fitzgerald song, my breath caught. "You remembered."

"I couldn't forget if I tried," he stated. "This is the same playlist we had sex to the night we conceived our son. I remember you telling me during a dark time in your life, her music gave you comfort. You never told me why though."

"Her song was the first actual music I heard," I explained. "In the hotel I stayed at in Europe after being rescued, they were playing this music in the elevator. I was hiding in a suitcase at the time, but it brought me comfort. An escape I never thought I'd have."

Pharaoh's eyes didn't leave mine as he gathered his hair and secured it atop of his head, removing his shirt next, his brilliantly brown body glistening under the candlelight.

"You mentioned yesterday that Duchess saved you from the camp."

I nodded, trying to focus on answering the question, momentarily distracted by how slowly he removed his belt, even the act of watching the leather slide through the denim belt loops intoxicatingly addictive. "She did," I finally confirmed. "From what I was told, Duchess and my mom split up to find me by going to two different countries. When my mom finally got a viable lead, Duchess was the closest to me. Instead of waiting for my mom to assist, her and a few others acted quickly and got me out of there. Honestly, I'm grateful she even found me, since in the camp they addressed us as numbers, not by name. Even tatted the numbers on us like we were property instead of people. I didn't decide on a name until after I was reunited with my mom and she told me she had wanted to name me Genesis, which meant the origin or beginning of something new."

"Is that why you got the tattoo on your neck?" he asked. "It's the only one you have, so I assume it covers the number."

"It does. Number one-twenty-two means nothing to me anymore, but this symbol is everything. Do you know the meaning?"

He smirked. "You already know I know what the fuck it means. I always thought it was symbolic that my name is Egyptian as is the Ankh symbol on your neck, representing the key of life."

I swallowed. "I thought that was coincidental when we met, too. Especially considering you have that symbol as a part of the tattoo design on your back."

"Nothing with us is coincidental, Ginx." He removed his jeans and boxers, his thick, prominent dick bouncing out now that it was free of confinement. "Meeting you taught me to believe in fate and the realization that your relationships and marriages will fail if you haven't found the person you're meant to be with. Or, in our case, if the timing is fucked up and I have to wait for your ass to realize you ain't in this shit alone."

"It's hard to feel like I'm not," I told him, my eyes slightly tearing. "I feel like I've been battling my entire life to survive, to feel worthy of a family, of my incredible son … of you."

"You're more than worthy of me," he muttered, looking like a lion about to slay their prey with the hungry gleam in his eyes as he mounted the bed and tossed both my legs over his strong shoulders. "I'm the one who will spend the rest of my life proving that I am worthy of being the partner, the protector, and the provider you need." The tip of his tongue flicked my clit. "But since you've always been a badass who ain't need no man to make her feel worthy, how about tonight, I make you a promise to always help you release the emotions and responsibilities you've carried around your entire life." He flicked it again, and I gasped.

"I'll be the reminder that underneath all that strength and reliability, you are a woman with needs and wants. A woman who can be vulnerable, and not look weak. Who can be emotional, and not be concerned that it makes her less than any man. A woman who can change the way a nationality treats their women by stepping in her purpose."

"I'll never be accepted by any Russian relatives, nor do I seek that."

"I know you don't. And accepted? Probably not," he said. "Respected, you damn sho' betta believe that shit will happen, especially after we kill your half-brother."

Talk about killing shouldn't have been my love language, but at the moment, his words were making love to my ears. And not just my need for justice, but everything he'd said before that, too.

I wiggled on the bed, bucking my hips a little, hoping to feel his tongue again. "Pharaoh, I'm already more aroused than I've ever been. It'll get embarrassing if you don't do something about it."

"Never be embarrassed." His hands roamed all over my body, long arms reaching my breasts, massaging my nipples while his head remained between my legs. "With me, Ginx, you can be whoever the hell you want to be."

Lick. Suckle. Lick.

My clit was already throbbing by the time he assured, "And I'll be the nastiest muthafucka I can be for you."

His tongue dove into my pussy, and I shamelessly screamed into the ceiling, too stimulated to do anything else. He always applied just the right pressure to my clit, and tonight was no different as he alternated between flicking my nub and licking my walls like a starved man lapping up a melting ice cream cone on a hot summer day.

My hips met the stroke of his tongue, the mixture of his saliva with my wetness causing a beautiful mess that I didn't even mind was ruining my sheets because I needed this. Needed *him*. And I was learning that it was okay to need someone else and not carry the weight of the world on your shoulders alone. Tonight, something in the air had changed between us. An agreement of sorts that from now on, it was us always. We were a team. A unit.

I burst into a brilliant mass of stars and rainbows and sunshine, momentarily losing my eyesight, then laughing in disbelief after gaining it back because apparently, being with him this way made me feel everything all at once.

By the time his dick filled me, the moment so beautifully overwhelming it brought tears to my eyes, I was already on the road to another quick orgasm.

"Go ahead and give me that shit," he provoked, referring to the second orgasm he craved from me.

I gave him what he requested, sounding like a damn banshee by the time he busted a nut right after, holding me by my shoulders to make sure his dick was so secured in my pussy that I didn't move.

Pharaoh didn't miss a beat, barely taking a break. He looked downright dangerous, the fire in his eyes only more intense as he cursed and talked dirty to me, his hair falling from the band that was holding it together, giving me something to grip onto when he sat me on top of his lap. If I was hurting him, he didn't say, both of us wild with lust, love, and all that nasty shit in between, our fucking on a whole other level, but so damn necessary for the release we both deserved.

By the third round, he slowed it down, peppering my sweaty body with kiss after sultry kiss, whispering, "I love you," after each one.

The way he made love to me that round, kissing away my tears and allowing me to release all the tragedies and hardships of my past, was almost too much for me to handle.

Intense.

Purposeful.

Powerful.

When most of your life had been spent littered in painful circumstances and surrounded by so much insecurity about your future, it was easy to start to wonder if you didn't deserve happiness. Pure elation didn't come easy for some, myself included. Yet, in this moment with him, life felt pretty fucking perfect.

I felt deserving of everything I was experiencing, and for the first time in my life, I held onto the idea that this was just the beginning. It hadn't been *our* time before. However, here and now belonged to *us*.

CHAPTER 13

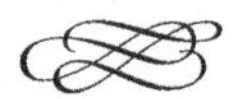

Fuck Questions, Shoot First

GENESIS

In one way or another, I'd been fighting my entire life. In prison camp, I was one of the toughest girls in there. Oftentimes, my fights had been with the boys, not the girls. I learned early on, fight or get fucked up.

When my mom married Noble Sr., it came with another host of problems because the Brooks family had been long-standing enemies of the Pierce family, Pharaoh's birth parents.

Joining Duchess and Stan at the academy by working as a liaison to try and build a better understanding between the different mafia families and shut down unlawful prison camps had been a whole other kind of battle.

However, none of that compared to the struggles I'd faced for the opportunity to hold a 9mm caliber to the head of the man responsible for kidnapping your loved one.

"Tell me what the fuck did you do with my mother?" I demanded, my tone firm.

As he had the past two hours, Boris remained quiet. Although myself and the Crownes had prepared for a battle, surprisingly, we caught Boris and his crew off guard, the intel from our kids proving that the academy was already molding the youth to think smarter and quicker than generations prior.

However, we hadn't known just how many more men had arrived from Russia, proving Boris had been planning something big. When we arrived at the underground tunnel—thirty feet below Chicago's pedway system—in the wee hours of the morning, Boris and his men were vulnerable and spread out between three tunnels that were connected by a central hub.

Jedidiah and Hollis, along with some of Jedidiah's men, had headed east down the tunnel, running into a few hiccups when Jedidiah recognized one of the men having worked together to bring down a mutual enemy years ago. Unfortunately, they were on different sides, and when friend was pinned against friend, Jackie D came out victorious.

Saint, Nash, a few of Saint's guys and fellow Drifters from his cleaning crew headed west. They had it the easiest, only coming into contact with a few men before they made light work at clearing the east tunnel, heading to the west to help Jackie D and Hollis after that.

Pharaoh, Jock, Keon, Cash, and I had gone after Boris

and his right-hand goons, Keon, Cash, and Jock quick to shoot two of Boris' largest men who they were sure were responsible for the deaths of two of their own, Jake and Jeremy. A few of Boris' men begged for mercy in Russian, but I was the only one who understood them. Jock, Cash, and Keon shot them, too; I wasn't even sure if it would've made a difference if they'd understood the men's plea.

Boris was waiting for us by the time we reached the main back room, smirking despite his defeat. I'd never seen him in person, only seen pictures. Yet, in person, he looked even more ruthless, his reputation for showing no mercy, even to his own people, evident in the bodies we'd found in their torture chamber.

The Crownes weren't surprised to find documents on Boris' desk detailing his partnership with Ronan and Eric McKay. They already knew they'd been betrayed by them, the evidence clear in the photos my contact had taken. Duchess was adamant to her children about them being careful in how they approached Ronan and McKay since the motives of both parties teaming up with Boris were muddy.

My mom was nowhere in the tunnels, and I figured if she was still alive, she wouldn't be, but I still held out hope for any indication she'd once been there. I came up short and found nothing.

However, we did find a young boy chained to one of the beds in a back room when scavenging the tunnels for clues. He looked hungry, scared, but like Boris, he spoke English, so I was able to communicate with him for the others to hear.

"How old are you?"

"I just turned twelve," the boy said, his lips cracked and his young, hazel eyes miserable.

"What's your name?" I asked.

"Dmitry."

I knelt down beside him, wanting to comfort him in some way despite the fact that I shouldn't. "Hi, Dmitry. You can call me Nee. I'm not here to hurt you, but if we take off this chain, you have to promise not to try anything funny."

"If you do, we'll kill you," Cash added, earning him a shove in the shoulder from Keon.

Dmitry's eyes were wide in fear. "O-Okay."

Right as we released him, a guard we thought we'd killed upon entering the room, raised his gun from the hallway. But he didn't shoot at us. He was aiming for Dmitry. Cash shot the man dead in the forehead before he could pull the trigger.

Dmitry looked from the guard to me and Cash, who he was standing between, and hugged us both. I was surprised, but Cash looked downright shocked considering he'd just threatened to kill the kid moments before.

"Can I go with you guys?" he asked.

I didn't have the heart to tell him he was our prisoner, under our protection but not free to go, until we figured out what to do with him, so instead I said, "Sure you can."

He looked relived. "Thank you. If I stay here, he'll kill me."

"Who?" Pharaoh asked.

"Boris," Dmitry answered. "He's my dad, but he hates me because I'm not like him."

My heart broke at his words, the similarity between our stories uncanny. I wasn't sure why Boris hated him, but being disliked or unwanted by a parent was a tough pill to swallow. At first glance in the darkened room, I just assumed he was a kid of one of Boris' enemies, not his own son. *Which makes me his aunt.*

"If Boris is your father, why did the guard try to kill you?" Pharaoh asked, sizing up the kid.

Dmitry glanced nervously around the room.

"It's okay," I told him in a calming voice. "You can tell us."

"All I know is that Boris only married my mother to gain power of overseeing her family and becoming my grandfather's successor. But when my grandfather died and my mother was killed, Boris learned everything was promised to me instead. He never liked me, but that's when the torture started." Dmitry dropped his head. "I'm not like him and he knows it. He wants me to be ruthless, and in his eyes, I'm too soft. So instead, he's stolen everything that's supposed to be mine, but he can't kill me because he needs me for access."

That's how Boris got so powerful without Igor's support. Stealing Dmitry's birthright.

Dmitry glanced at the dead guard. "All the guards were ordered to kill me if we were losing an attack. I hope this means Boris is dead."

"Not yet," I answered.

"Do you know much about your father's business?" Pharaoh asked.

He nodded. "The walls down here aren't as thick as they seem, and the ones back in Moscow are even thinner."

I looked to Pharaoh, both of us noting his honesty when the situation called more for lies than truth.

It took us three hours to wrap things up and head to the Illinois countryside to one of the properties Pharaoh owned, deeper underground than the tunnels had been as we tried to get answers from Boris. Easier said than done when trying to interrogate and threaten a man who didn't care about anything other than his reign of power and had nothing to lose at this point.

* * *

PHARAOH

Eventually, we had to leave Boris alone with only water and bread once a day for two months before we even got him to speak, and only then was it because he was pissed that we lied and said we killed Dmitry.

"You are a disgrace to Russians everywhere," Boris spat, cursing Genesis out in Russian and English. "I made my own son a prisoner for the better good, but you're too soft and weak like Igor was. You'll never find your mother if you don't even have the courage to kill your greatest enemy. When I escape, I'll spend the rest of my life making sure you and your family pay."

I wanted to kill that muthafucka right then and there, especially since he cared more about power than his child. Yet, he'd given us more intel about Esi than ever before in his rant, including indicating we'd never find her, which meant she was still alive somewhere. Ginx picked up clues in his native language that led her to figure out a few locations he frequented.

When it came to Dmitry, we reached out to his mother's family, seizing an opportunity for us to build an alliance with one of the most powerful families in Moscow.

Dmitry assured us he had a good relationship with his aunt and uncle and they could be trusted, but I was apprehensive about the entire situation. Cash was a major reason we began trusting Dmitry more, the pair bonding in a way none of us saw coming. For all the years I'd known him, Cash had always claimed he was never meant to be anyone's father, yet Dmitry was proving Cash just be talking bullshit sometimes.

Dmitry's aunt and uncle didn't feel like it was safe enough for him to return to Russia, even with Boris out of the picture. It was decided that Dmitry would attend Couronne d'Ombre with Noble, Christian, and Trinity, which was where he was now.

"I can't thank you enough," she told Brielle, hugging the stealth spy with the rich melanin skin tone and huge highlighted blonde and brown curls tightly. Turns out, Brielle had been the one to help Ginx get intel on Boris arriving to America, and now she'd gotten more information based off the latest intel Genesis had given her.

Brielle's sister had also gone missing a few years ago, around the same time Carmen did. Genesis had told me that she'd been away from Noble for an entire year at one point to follow-up on a lead they had about Brielle's sister. A lead that almost costs them both their lives. The trail was a dead end and Brielle was still searching for her sister as we were Carmen. In my heart, I still held out hope that we'd find them.

"You know I always got your back, Nee." Brielle turned to me and bumped fists. "It's nice meeting the man who I've been hearing about foreverrrrrrr."

"Girl, shut up," Genesis told her, lightly shoving her.

"So, when the hell where you gonna tell me you're also a spy?" I asked after Brielle left us alone on the rooftop of The Congress Hotel—one of our favorite places to get some peace and quiet.

The Drake Hotel was still the place I preferred to do business meetings, but The Congress Hotel was my latest stash house, or better yet, stash hotel, that I'd acquired. The staff and management, they all worked for me now in one way or another.

Nothing compared to the way I'd set up the rooftop of The Congress Hotel. What looked like a regular hotel roof on the outside had plenty of discreet spots now that I'd concealed off.

She shrugged. "I'm not a spy per say. At least not in this country, so it doesn't really matter, right?"

I laughed, pulling her to me. "Ginx, a spy is a spy no matter what country. I thought we said no more secrets."

She smacked her lips. "Boy, please. I haven't been doing any entertaining spy shit in forever. I've been boring. Or did you forget I've been at the academy and tracking Boris in Russia?"

"Of course I ain't forget. All of that still seems like some spy shit."

"Plus, I could have sworn I told you I was born in the UK."

"Nah," I shook my head, "you said your mom was born in the UK. You ain't say shit about having dual citizenship."

She batted her long, dark brown lashes. "What can I say, I'm a complicated woman."

"Biggest fucking understatement." I kissed her tattoo, loving the way she moaned when I did. "So what the fuck are you gonna do to make it up to me for keeping another secret?"

"I like to think keeping you on your toes is good enough."

"Fuck that." I looked around for the outdoor bin I paid one of The Congress Hotel staff good money to keep stocked for me. "You know what to do."

Her body shivered. "But it's cold as hell. We shouldn't even be up here in the fall."

"If you're so damn cold, why'd you wear a dress today then?"

"It's a long sweater dress," she defended. "Appropriate for this weather."

I ain't say shit after that, but I gave her a look that let her know to stop fucking with me. Rolling her eyes, she popped open the bin and pulled out one of the blankets that was tossed on top. Now that Genesis and I were together, life had been … interesting, but in a good way. Mentally, she got me better than anyone in my life. Emotionally, I shared some deep shit with her. Secrets I thought I would take to the grave. Physically, we enjoyed each other on every level.

Our relationship wasn't just about the physical, but her dress hiked up to her hips, panties slid to the side, legs spread all the way eagle style so that sweet pussy of hers could wink at me was my favorite way to look at her. Just like she was now.

"Spread 'em more," I directed, motioning my hands back and forth for her to widen her legs.

"That's as far as they go," she muttered.

"Bullshit." Leaning down, I slid a hand up and down her slit. "Don't nobody know your pussy betta than I do, so don't be stingy wit' it."

She rolled her eyes again, smacking her lips this time as she spread them to their brink.

"You had betta listen," I mumbled.

Her lips parted. "That shit ain't funny.

"Wasn't nobody playin' Ginx." To show her how serious I was, I didn't give her time to say shit else as I dropped to my knees and gripped her thighs, deep diving my tongue into her wet and hungry pussy.

She squealed and squirmed, but I kept her locked in place, loving the way she was always so damn responsive even if she did give me a hard time.

Genesis came in record time, convulsing all around my

tongue, not giving a damn who could hear her. I didn't expect her to return the favor, but I didn't stop her when she dropped to all fours, her dress falling back around her and blocking my view of her pussy, but giving me a great one of her mouth on my dick.

I'd only planned for us to have a quickie because we had several meetings we had to get to. Yet, once I got started, I didn't want to stop, obsessed with how warm and right she felt.

I ended up fucking her on that rooftop until the sun came up.

Brought her back to my place and fucked her again.

Admired her naked body without clothes or a pistol on deck.

Let her run her fingers and tongue all over my tatted body. No Glock needed.

Turned my spare room to mirror the one at Delilah.

Watched her show me what the fuck she could do without an audience.

Talked to her about a threesome that she quickly turned down.

Lost my shit when I realized she turned it down because she planned to surprise me with a threesome instead.

Realized she was way freakier than I was when it came to some shit.

Reminded her why my face will always be her throne.

Learned how to give a pussy facial since I cherished her shit and the amount of sex we had was too damn much for any woman, even a vixen like Ginx.

Put her ass on a pussy facial break when I kept coming home to her legs wide open and all the spa products laid out for me.

Convinced her ass to just move in with me since she was over all the damn time.

Introduced her to all my kids.

Vowed never to have all my baby mommas with her in the same room again (two claps to any nigga who was able to handle that shit, 'cause I ain't like it).

Had "the talk" about birth control because she wasn't sure she wanted more kids, but was still deciding.

Told her I support her regardless. Because let's be for real, I had enough of 'em for both of us.

Took extreme measures of torturing Boris who really was a grimy muthafucka.

Met Destiny and Adrian, Genesis' friends.

Made plans to vacation with them.

Told 'em I planned to marry her one day when she was ready.

Held her while she cried about still not finding her mom.

Convinced her we would.

Promised myself I'd do whatever I could to never see her hurt like that again a day in my life.

Prepared myself for the outcome that not finding Esi may send Ginx in a spiral she couldn't come back from.

Took her on a date after realizing it had been a while and we ain't even fuck until after we'd been out for twelve hours, loving the city we met in and spending time just shooting the shit about any and everything. Wasn't sure when Ginx stopped being my unlucky charm. Probably never was. In a way, I feel like I always knew we'd end up together, it just took us a while to get here.

"Pharaoh!" she screamed, her second orgasm hitting swift and fast as I made love to her at five o'clock in the morning since Ginx had a thing for sunrise sex. Hearing her scream my name was the highlight of every day we spent together. The best part was, I could go the rest of my life doing any and everything I could to hear it.

Ours wasn't the typical kind of love. It was messy. It didn't make sense at times. It was complicated as hell and a muthafucka was still learning how to love her right and the way she needed, just like she was working on loving me the same way. But the shit was ours nonetheless.

For the good.

Better.

Worst.

And more importantly, for all those get-the-fuck-outta-here and I-know-you-fuckin'-lyin' moments in between.

EPILOGUE

Fuck Vulnerability, Strap Up

Some weeks later ...

PHARAOH

I'D NEVER BEEN the type of muthafucka to leave the city much. While my siblings were busy working here and there, traveling for business and pleasure as much as they could, I mainly traveled between Chicago and Mexico.

I never cared too much about not being as cultured or worldly as the rest of my family. I had a place in the city. A legacy to protect. If I was out of town, who would make sure shit ran right? Who would protect what was ours … what we'd built?

With the opening of the remaining gentlemen lounges as a result of the app already helping us locate several frequenters of one of the largest human trafficking galas in the nation and Genesis' quest to locate her mother, I'd been more places in a few months than I had in decades.

Who would have thought a muthafucka from my hood would be where I was today, especially when it seemed like my choices were to go pro, go to prison, or go to hell on a silver platter if I got popped off.

"Pops, you finally ready to tell us why we're all here?" Zayden asked.

I glanced around the table at my older kids who I'd requested come over, leaving the younger three out of the discussion because they were too young. "Yeah, why don't y'all gather around the table." I motioned, pointing to the large, rectangular table I'd gotten specifically for when I had all my kids over.

"Oh shit," Seyra, my oldest daughter, exclaimed. "If you took out the good silver platters and had the estate's chef, Figgy, bring all this food over here, you must be about to tell us something important."

Noble stopped eating the blueberry muffin he'd grabbed from the table. "So this isn't a normal spread for a Sunday, huh?"

Porter, Seyra's brother and my oldest son, shook his head. "Nah, bruh. Dad only does the Godfather type of setup when he got some serious shit to say and he wants our undivided attention."

"That's why we left our phones at the door," my other son, Orion, stated. "Too much of a distraction."

I pointed to him, because he liked people to focus when he spoke like I did. He knew me well. All my kids did, and it was something I actively strived to do by letting them be as accessible to me as possible. Even now, several of them were crashing at my house, and there wasn't a time when my house didn't have at least one of my kids living with me for one reason or another.

"And if any of us had brought our laptops, he would have confiscated those, too," my daughter, Emery, added. She was the artistic one of the group. Always writing. Always drawing. Always in a book or laptop.

"I don't care what Dad does," Kenia interjected, our resident foodie and the first one to have every item on the table in her plate. "Y'all can't tell me he don't always have the best food for these family meetings, *and* we get to leave with to-go plates."

"That's right, baby girl," I said with a smile. Kenia wasn't the youngest, but she'd always be baby girl to me.

"Kiss ass," my other daughter, Sloan, muttered, entering the dining room with my son, Tobias.

Those two had always been close and probably caused me the most panic attacks with their rebellious ways and trouble that they always got into.

"You both are late."

Sloan shrugged. "The bus took forever to pick us up."

"Next time, let me know and I'll send a car."

"Understood," Tobias answered, giving Sloan a look.

My best guess why Tobias ain't want me to get riled up? He'd gotten kicked out of school … again.

"Let's get to it," I announced, clasping my hands together. "I called you all here to talk about the future."

"Oh shit," Seyra mumbled. "You for real serious. I can hear it in your voice."

"Is everything good with the business?" Porter asked.

"It is," I told them. "But this is less about my future and more about yours. You know, I'm getting older, and although I've always encouraged each of you to go after the life you want, I need to know how this family's legacy fits into your future."

"What do you mean?" Emery asked.

"For example, I've known since you were little that you'd be an artist and you can spot a painting a mile away and tell me the creator, the year it was painted, and the last owner of that painting."

She nodded. "Yeah, I'm definitely like that."

"There's also more to that, right?"

Emery's eyes widened at the question, searching my face in disbelief. "How could you know that?"

"Know what?" Seyra asked.

"It's not my business to tell, it's Emery's and she doesn't have to share."

"I'm the one who stole that twenty-thousand-dollar painting from The Art Institute," she blurted, placing her face in her hands. "And it's not the first one."

"Shut the fuck up!" Kenia exclaimed. "My friends have all been talking about the person behind that, and here I am, sister's with an art thief." Kenia enthusiastically clapped her hands. I knew what Kenia had been up to as well, but I didn't have that kind of time to get into it.

I turned to Orion, who was already looking at me and laughing. "What is it?"

"You already know what I do, too, huh?" he asked.

I nodded. "Yeah, you leave a trademark with yo' shit, so we'll have to talk about how you can be more discreet."

"Man, whateva." He waved me off. "I learned from the best how to move around money without being seen."

"And yo' cocky ass can still learn more," I told him. "Same with you, Seyra, only yo' shit is legal here now. But I still know someone you can talk to in order to perfect your edible's business." I'd recently met Carter's sister-in-law, Jordyn, and we'd hit off. Reminded me of Seyra in a lot of ways.

"I'd love that, Dad," she said with a smile.

"Okay, so you know what we've been up to on the side, but you can't be mad, right?" Zayden asked. "We learned how to embrace our skills through you."

"I'm not mad," I clarified. "Just the opposite." I looked to each of them. "I've tried my best to always be there for you kids, but as a parent, it's sometimes difficult to juggle everything."

"And our moms don't make it easy," Seyra added.

"They don't." I laughed. "But I want you to have the opportunity to learn what you can while I'm still here to see you learn it and help you along the way. I've been honest with you all about the school that Noble attends. And the opportunity stands that if any of you want to go, you have that option."

Sloan and Tobias looked to each other, and Noble tapped Zayden on the arm.

"What about those of us who are older and already in the family business?" Porter asked.

"You can continue working with me and going about your life like you have, or we can talk more about what you really want to do in your future." I truly looked at Porter, noting the slight relief in his features and the way he rubbed his hands together. Being my oldest son, he'd always felt obligated to work with me, and no matter how many times I told him he didn't have to, in some way or another, he did. He had his own life and goals. A girlfriend he loved. A kid who adored him.

It would take a while for him to step into his purpose, but following in his father's footsteps wasn't what he wanted to do. He just didn't realize it yet.

"Basically, I just want each of you to know that the

choice is and always has been yours. I'm here for guidance. I'm here for advice. I'm available for anything you want to learn. And Shadow Crowne was created by your family, so you each have a right to get educated there if you want. As always, there are some things that go on in this family that you can't discuss with your mothers, or your stepfathers, your partners, or your kids if you have them. What goes on in this family, stays in this family. When I'm long gone, you'll have each other, and blood is not what connects you. Love and heart do."

I'd been giving the same speech for years, and in a way, I was sure most of them were sick of it. Not today though. As I observed my sons and daughters, watching each of their minds work, I couldn't help but feel a sense of pride to be in all their lives. It didn't matter if they were biologically mine or not, they were my kids all the same.

Noble nodded, wearing a smile and glancing around at his siblings like he was finally able to spend some quality time with the family he'd waited fourteen years to meet. Siblings that I was grateful accepted him without a second thought.

Seyra dabbed the corners of her eyes while Porter nodded, looking more relaxed than I'd seen him in a while. Each of them were lost in their thoughts, but as we all got to eating—thanks to Kenia reminding us that good food was still on the table—I reminded myself that I was the lucky muthafucka who was blessed to have this crew carry on my legacy in ways I was sure I didn't even see coming yet.

* * *

GENESIS

It may have taken a while, but we lucked up when Brielle called to tell me she'd gotten a tip that my mother, Esi, was being held captive in Romania. Up until now, I had mainly been searching in Russia.

I had no idea how beautiful the Romanian countryside was, but we weren't here for pleasure. We were here to get my mother back.

"I hope this works," I muttered, more to myself than anyone standing around the small, metal table in our Romanian hideout. We'd been in the country for two days making sure the plan we'd created back in the States was still the best plan of action now that we were here.

"My guys are ready," Jedidiah confirmed, tapping his first lieutenant, Ice, who was going to lead the team to distract the Romanian soldiers guarding the entrance to a historic castle where my mom was being held captive.

Boris must have known I would never think to search a tourist destination for her, and although we were implementing our rescue mission at night to avoid as many tourists as possible, we still had to tread lightly.

"I reached out to my guy, and he'll hold off the cops as long as he can," Pharaoh stated, looking around the table. Being in the drug game for as long as he had, Pharaoh had contacts in a lot of places.

"Brielle will meet us there with the others," I announced.

"Who is Brielle again?" Saint asked. He and his men, along with Hollis and Creed, had all come to help us on this mission. Honestly, I was so grateful for the Crownes it almost brought tears to my eyes in gratitude. Especially Saint since Taraj had just given birth to a beautiful baby boy.

"We worked together to expose a prison camp," I explained. "She's good at getting information and remaining unseen. She prefers to work alone, but she has friends here and they are all willing to help."

"Esi is important to quite a few of Genesis and Brielle's friends who are assisting," Pharaoh explained, proving that he really did listen to everything I told him. "She's been there for them in one way or another, and right now, we need all the help we can get."

"And we should probably get going," I announced. "Are you all ready?"

Everyone nodded, polishing their knives, grabbing their weapons, and making sure their guns were loaded. We headed out in separate unlicensed vehicles as discussed. Brielle called me along the way to let me know that her and a couple others had already arrived and were inside. I wasn't surprised. Stealing a prized artifact held in the museum section of the castle would be a piece of cake for Brielle, but an added distraction on top of the others we had planned.

Multiple diversions were exactly what we needed to get in undetected, a few of Saint's guys being the only ones to run into trouble. As we had been before, I was with Pharaoh, Jock, Keon, and Cash.

"Heads up!" Cash warned, as we came across some of guards. We left Keon and Cash behind to deal with them as the three of us moved forward. It took fifteen minutes to get to the spot she was being held, and it was clear that with Boris captured, security hadn't been as tight as we suspected. Jock was able to handle three guards on his own, and Pharaoh and I handled the other five.

"Go ahead," Pharaoh encouraged, tossing me the keys he'd gotten off another guard that came out of nowhere. I ran quick and fast down the narrow hallway, knowing from Brielle's intel that if my mom was still alive, this was where she was at.

My finger stumbled to undo the lock. However, the moment I opened that door and saw my beautiful yet battered mother looking up at me with her fierce, brown eyes, I couldn't help but burst into tears.

"Mom, I can't believe I found you," I whispered, helping her out of the chains.

She gently cupped my face. "Sweetie, I never doubted you would. That's what kept me alive."

We took off down the hallway I'd come, me holding her up since it was clear she hadn't walked in a while.

Pharaoh was a sight for sore eyes when he met us in the hallway, a few cuts on his face, but otherwise, good to go.

"Jock had to go back and help Cash and Keon, but I'm getting you both out of here," he said, lifting my mom with ease as the three of us took off. Leaving was much easier than coming as the path had been cleared by others who'd arrived to help us.

I didn't release the breath I was holding until we were back in the car driving to our hideout. Based off the updates I was hearing in the earpiece, we had a few injuries, but no one was killed. *Thank God.* Everyone had decided to help knowing the risks, but my heart couldn't take it if someone lost their life on my mission.

When we got back to the hideout, Pharaoh let me have some time alone with my mom as he and Jedidiah went to handle business. She needed a hospital, but that would wait until we got back to the States tomorrow.

"You brought Boris with you, didn't you?" she asked.

I nodded. "He isn't here, but another location. And, Mom, before you ask me to show him mercy, just know that I nor Pharaoh will listen."

My mom briefly leaned her forehead to mine before kissing my cheek, making sure she had my attention when she said, "Baby, I've been waiting for you and that man to find your way back to each other for years."

"Really?"

"Yes, I have. Boris didn't kill me because he wanted me for leverage … not just to lure you to him, but also because of my Ghanaian family. Your family. True greed if I ever saw it. Little did he know, I had made my brother promise to never respond to a threat against my life. My career has always been dangerous, and I'll protect my family even if I haven't seen them in years."

My mom was born into Ghanaian royalty, but she left it all behind when she worked in foreign intelligence and left her community for a different life. It didn't change what was in her blood though … or what ran through mine. She later discovered more history and learned her mother was from a long line of Ghanaian warriors.

"So what you're saying is—"

"I hope that man of yours kills that son of a bitch," she finished. "If he doesn't, I will."

I hugged her tightly, never wanting to let go. She wouldn't have to kill Boris though. Pharaoh was going to handle it, and it wasn't lost on me that by the end of the night, he would have killed two of my brothers … for different reasons, but killed them all the same.

A part of me was slightly bothered by it, but not really. Not like I should be. Pharaoh would do anything to protect his family, and after everything we'd been through, I was his now. I was sure of that. And it wasn't just because we shared a child, it was because we'd chosen each other long before either of us even realized it.

My mom could see it, too. When Pharaoh and Jedidiah returned, Pharaoh pulled me to him and gave me a kiss that definitely should have been done in private before he hugged my mom tightly and told her he was glad we had her back and that she could stay with us until she had everything figured out, or indefinitely if she preferred.

"Oh, he's a good one," my mom whispered. She'd stay for a while, but I knew my mother. She would be onto the next adventure after she healed.

Later that night, we enjoyed an impromptu party that Hollis had decided to throw in celebration by inviting everyone who had helped saved my mom and having us all take shots of Hennessey at the fact that none of our people had been killed.

Was having a party in our small hideout reckless? Yeah.

Did I dare anyone to mess with a Crowne? Only if they didn't care about their life.

Even as the party died down and folks lay in the small hideout drunk in any corner they could find, I knew that life couldn't get much better than this. We'd rescued my mom. My son was safe at school. And I had this sexy, drop-dead gorgeous, make-me-wanna-bite-my-bottom-lip man laying across my lap while he slept soundly as the sun came up.

I needed to rest, too. However, I just watched him, too deliriously happy to do anything except run my fingers through his dreads and thank God that for now, our story had a happy ending.

"Three months," he said in his sleep. Or at least I thought he had still been asleep until his eyes opened.

"Three months until what?" I asked.

"Until we get married," he stated, so matter-of-factly I had to laugh.

"Boy, you crazy."

"I'm dead ass." He pulled out a brilliant diamond ring from his pocket that was in the shape of my Ankh tattoo.

"I've never seen anything like this," I told him, letting him slip it on my finger.

"I had it custom made." He sat up and faced me. "I wanted to propose to yo' ass a while ago, but we had to find your mom first and I needed to make sure I had Noble's permission."

I smiled. "You asked him for his blessing?"

"Yeah, I called him at school and that little shit told me he had to think about it. Had me waiting a whole goddamn week for his response."

"He's something else."

"Stubborn like his mama," he said. "He finally told me he was happy for us and couldn't imagine you with anyone else."

"I can't either," I said, placing a soft kiss on his lips.

"Well shit, is that a yes then?"

I laughed. "That's a hell fucking yesssssss! I'll marry you and become stepmom to your busload of kids."

His smile dropped. "Yo, that shit ain't funny."

"It is."

"A busload though." He shook his head. "A big van maybe, but not a bus."

"A small school bus, baby, but it's okay. I love them, and I love you." I kissed him deeper this time to ease the teasing, but leave it to Hollis to interrupt the mood.

"Congrats!" he said, yawning as he woke up from the chair he'd crashed on. "Genesis, did Patrón ever tell you about the rap we re-created for him?"

I looked from him to Pharaoh. "Nah, this is news to me."

"Oh, you gotta hear this shit." Hollis pulled out his phone.

"I ain't even tell y'all about Genesis, so she wasn't mentioned in the damn video," Pharaoh spat.

"That's what makes this shit even better," Hollis claimed. "We're saving her the trouble of making a spreadsheet of your exes." He pressed play, avoiding Pharaoh's outstretched arm as he tried to snatch the phone.

"Bae, you don't wanna hear that shit."

I laughed as the first lines played. "Oh hell yeah I do."

Saint woke up and stood on the other side of Hollis, all three of us watching the small phone. By the end of the video me, my mama, and anyone who had woken up were laughing.

"Oh my God, I don't even know what to say," I mentioned, trying to hold back my laughs and failing.

"On the morning I propose, that's when you decide to show her this shit?" Pharaoh growled. "You know that's fucked up, right?"

"Baby, I don't care about your past and I know who I'm marrying," I told him, planting kisses all over his face and trying to get him to stop glaring at Hollis.

"Imma kill that dude," he said. "Always playin' and shit."

Pharaoh was annoyed the entire plane ride home. Me, on the other hand, I had already gotten Hollis to airdrop the video to me.

I wasn't the jealous type, but clearly, I had to keep track of the women Pharaoh had dated over the years. You never know when a random ex may pop up at a Crowne function claiming him to be the father of their child.

That shit happens.

I was proof.

BONUS SCENE

Introducing Académie de la Couronne de l'Ombre (Shadow Crown Academy)

PHARAOH

My kids had watched Harry Potter when they were younger, but I would have paid more attention to that shit if I'd known I'd be walking into a similar place.

"It's beautiful," I said aloud, glancing around the property at all the tall trees with the sun peeking through every now and then. "I can't believe how secluded it is."

When Stan and Duchess asked me and Genesis to accompany them on a visit to the school, I couldn't pass up the chance. Genesis knew all about the academy, but I was still learning. Still soaking it all in.

"We need it to be," Duchess explained. "Originally, an academy like this was my father's idea."

"That Idris, not Elba, triflin' asshole," Queenie huffed. "Tricked me into marrying his charming ass. The dumb fucker."

"Mama, that was uncalled for."

Queenie shrugged. "What? He blessed me with a few kids, but you gotta admit, he was dumb as hell to leave all this." She waved her hands up and down her body, her wheelchair shaking when she did so.

Duchess rolled her eyes. "Anyway, my father was a complicated man, but he believed in a different education. As did his father and my great-grandfather. Couronne d'Ombre has existed in some way, shape, or form, just not on such a large scale."

"You really brought his vision to life," Genesis stated. "Every time I come to this place, I wish it existed when I was a kid."

"Me too, dear." Duchess motioned for us to sit in the promenade that was close to the center of campus. "As I mentioned back in Chicago, here at the academy, we are at the centerfold of the education. Criminals, thieves, heirs to their parents or grandparents' business or legacy. In a world where criminals control businessmen, businessmen control politicians, politicians control law enforcement, and law enforcement controls the people, it all starts with *us*."

"We hone the skills and traits that make our community great at what we do starting them young on a seven-pillar learning system," Stan added. "Whether your child is enrolled into the leadership division, enforcement chapter, or one of our other five pillars, they will understand the world they were born into and flourish. They will be taught different languages and perfect their fighting skills. At Shadow Crown, they are given the tools to succeed in a world that wants us to believe that we aren't important."

"When that couldn't be further from the truth," Duchess clarified. "Our students are the true definition of importance. Lifelong allies are made here. The children of enemies are forced to co-exist. What make our scholars Couronne d'Ombre is the fact that the shadows are where most of them will live … will blossom. The ones you never see making the decisions, but are right there in the centerfold."

I wasn't sure what came over me. Maybe it was the inspiring way Duchess and Stan talked about the academy or how enlightened I felt just being on the grounds that made me stand and close my eyes, taking in the smell. The sounds. The entire feel of the place in a way I hadn't really focused on anything in a while. When I opened my eyes, I saw Noble, Christian, and Trinity in the distance, watching us. I tossed Noble a head nod, which he returned, smiling before he left, my eyes only briefly catching sight of their backs as a bell rang.

"Here's the thing, son," Duchess stated, placing a hand on my shoulder as she looked toward the direction the kids had gone. "I want to be perfectly honest with you. Creed and Tristan were going to take over as headmasters of this place one day."

I turned back to the group, not surprised to find Creed had joined. He flew down with us, but I hadn't seen him since we'd gotten to the academy.

"It was always Tristan's vision," Creed explained when I met his stare. "Not mine. At least not with her by my side."

"We want you take over," Stan revealed. "Not now, but one day."

"The students already love Genesis," Duchess mentioned. "And you've always been a teacher at heart."

"Not a teacher," I denied. "Education has never been my thing."

"Not the traditional way of educating," Duchess corrected. "Whether it was teaching your kids, the people who work for you, or those that have followed after you and been loyal because of how *you* lead them. You've been teaching others how to navigate our world since you were ten years old. In a way, Stan and I saw our dream come to fruition when we met you." Duchess dabbed the corners of her eyes, the emotion I saw in them tugging at my heart-strings.

"Thank you for taking a chance on me." I hugged her tighter than I feel like I ever had before, and she let me, crying softly into my shoulder.

"Pharaoh, there was always so much more to you than what meets the eye, and that special something is what has made you a leader in this family since you were a kid."

When we broke our embrace, all eyes were on me.

"Come on." Stan nodded to the main hall. "There's someplace else we want to show you."

We all walked across the courtyard, into the main hall, and through several sets of large, iron double doors.

"We just renovated this section," Stan explained. "It hasn't even been revealed to anyone outside of us yet."

It seemed over thirty long tables were in the room and sunlight was shining through the stained-glass panels. We walked down the middle aisle, stopping when we reached two tall, black, steel chairs, with plush, black velvet cushions on them.

"We're still working on the decor, but you get the idea," Stan enlightened.

"It looks great in here," I pointed out as Duchess stopped between Genesis and I.

"Stan and I won't be here forever, but we feel like the legacy of Couronne d'Ombre lies with you." Duchess glanced to my right. "And strong, unbreakable Genesis."

Ginx reached out and squeezed Duchess' hand, tears in the corners of her eyes.

"Did you know about this?" I asked Genesis.

She shrugged, sporting a sly smirk when she told me, "It doesn't matter what I know or what I didn't know. All that matters is right now." She reached out her hands. "These chairs look like they were meant for us, don't they?"

"They do." Grabbing her hand, we walked up the short flight of stairs. "Shall we?"

"When you see a grand black throne, you must sit on it," she stated, both of us turning and taking a seat beside each other.

I couldn't deny that it felt damn good sitting there. It felt *right.* Like I wasn't just meant for the streets, but had an even higher purpose a muthafucka like me never even thought would be his reality.

"Well, what do you say, young buck?" Queenie asked. "You takin' over this joint or what?"

"I'll do it," I announced, squeezing Genesis' hand as I looked to the parents who I admired more than they probably realized. "Duchess, Stan, you both helped make me who I am, and I want to share that knowledge with others. When you're ready, we'll take over as headmasters of Shadow Crown Academy."

Duchess clasped her hands together and leaned into Stan, the two of them kissing, which I rarely saw them do when we were around. They loved each other, but seeing them this affectionate was proof that my response had meant a lot to them.

I felt like royalty on that throne. I'd always been a king in some way, but now I had my queen. My partner for life. I'd have to figure out who would take my place back home, but I needed to be patient while my kids figured their shit out. In the meantime, I wasn't just preparing to retire from my reign in the streets. Now, I was prepping for a whole new future and even more kids that I would be responsible for.

A new era.

New memories.

New wife since Genesis and I were getting married soon.

Who the hell am I kidding? I couldn't wait that long. As soon as we got back, I was dragging her ass to the city hall to lock this shit down.

The End

WOULD LOVE TO HEAR FROM YOU!

I hope you enjoyed Throne of a Pharaoh! More in the Crowne Legacy series coming soon! I love to hear from readers! Thanks in advance for any reviews, messages or emails :).

Save and Author! Leave a Review!

Stop by my online Coffee Corner and get the latest info on my books, contests, virtual events and more!

www.bit.ly/SherelleGreensCoffeeCorner

ABOUT THE AUTHOR

USA Today Bestselling and award-winning author, Sherelle Green, is a Chicago native with a dynamic imagination and a passion for reading and writing. To her family and friends, she's known as a hug connoisseur, dishing out as many warm hugs as she can. Reality television and lip gloss may be her guilty pleasures; however, she's in an unapologetic love affair with coffee. On many days, she can be found scouring different shops to add to her coffee mug collection or traveling the world for literary inspiration.

Sherelle loves connecting with readers and other literary enthusiasts and enjoys composing emotionally driven stories that are steamy, edgy, and touch on real life issues. Her overall goal is to create relatable and fierce heroines who are flawed, just like the strong and sexy heroes who fight so hard to win their hearts.

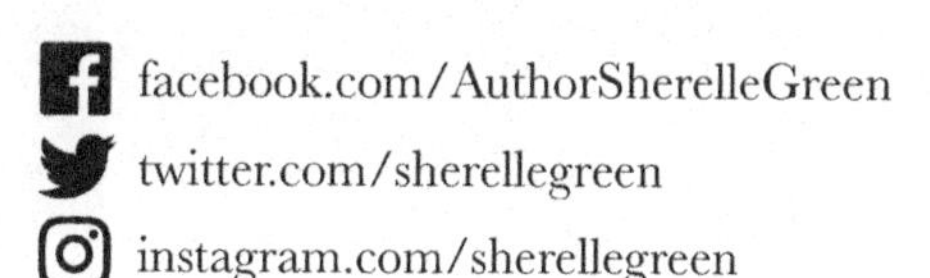

ALSO BY SHERELLE GREEN

Crowne Legacy:

Face Down Fridays

Sins of a Saint

Jedidiah's Crowning Glory

Love Always, Tristan

To Marry a Madden:

Blessed By Malakai

Claimed By Crayson

Caden's Situationship

Carter's Undoing

To Marry a Madden

Black Friday (Short spin-off)

Social Experiment Series:

Single AF

Bad Decisions Good Regrets

Fake News

Still Single AF

New Year Bae-Solutions (multi-author anthology):

Seven Month Drought

Once Upon a Bridesmaid, Baby & Funeral (multi-author anthology):

Yours Forever

Yours Ever After

Inspiring Dominic

High Class Society Series:

Blue Sapphire Temptation

Passionate Persuasion

Women of Park Manor (multi-author anthology):

Her Undeniable Distraction

Carnivale Chronicles (multi-author anthology):

Summer Kisses

Distinguished Gentlemen (multi-author anthology):

The Contingency Bid

Bare Sophistication Series:

Enticing Winter

Falling for Autumn

Waiting for Summer

Nights of Fantasy

Her Unexpected Valentine

Road to Forever

Her Christmas Wish

An Elite Event Series:

A Tempting Proposal

If Only for Tonight

Red Velvet Kisses (Micah Madden)

Beautiful Surrender (Malik Madden)

Additional Books:

A Los Angeles Passion

A Miami Affair

Wrapped in Red

FREE Online Short Stories:

One Last Chance

Our Season For Love

Made in the USA
Coppell, TX
04 August 2022